Cold in Summer

Cold in Summer

Tracy Barrett

Henry Holt and Company
New York

For Greg, who first told me about the wind that
blows cold in summer and warm in winter

Henry Holt and Company, LLC
Publishers since 1866
115 West 18th Street
New York, New York 10011
www.henryholt.com

Library of Congress Cataloging-in-Publication Data
Barrett, Tracy.
Cold in summer / Tracy Barrett.
p.   cm.
Summary: At the beginning of seventh grade, Ariadne moves to a Tennessee town near
a former farming community submerged under a man-made lake and meets the ghost
of a girl from the past.
[1. Ghosts—Fiction.   2. Moving, Household—Fiction.
3. Tennessee—Fiction.]   I. Title.
PZ7.B275355 Co 2003   [Fic]—dc21   2002067888

ISBN 0-8050-7052-4
First Edition—2003
Printed in the United States of America on acid-free paper. ∞

1   3   5   7   9   10   8   6   4   2

Cold in Summer

one

Ariadne flipped over, treading water, and tried to look down through the darkness. Her wet hair flopped over her eyes, and she couldn't spare a hand to push it back. It didn't matter. She couldn't even see her toes. What if she were right over an old barn? Could she cut herself on a thresher or a reaper? She had no idea what threshers and reapers were, but last year her sixth-grade social-studies book had said they were used on farms. They would probably still have sharp edges, even if they were covered with rust by now. The thought made her shudder, and she bent her legs until her treading knees nearly broke the surface.

Hector was facedown a few feet away, his arms wrapped around a boat cushion. His dark hair floated around his head like seaweed, and his back was already starting to turn pink. Ariadne swam over and grabbed a corner of the cushion.

"Hey!" Hector said, and loosened his grip. "You trying to drown me?"

"Let me hold on a second," said Ariadne. "I'm sinking."

"Fresh water is less buoyant than salt water," he said.

"I know, I know—spare me the science lecture," she said. It was annoying to hear her little brother use a word like *buoyant*. "Up to the Bs already?" She tossed her head to get her hair out of her eyes, and a strand caught in her mouth. She spat it out, grimacing at the muddy taste. "Where's Mom?" she asked.

"Back on shore with Dad." Hector jerked his head in their direction. "Now let go of my cushion. Get your own if you can't dog-paddle that far." Stung, Ariadne let go and swam with her best crawl toward the shore. She looked back to see if Hector was impressed with her form, but he had hugged the cushion to his chest again and was staring down, down into the depths, as though he could see something in the murk below his yellow swim trunks.

Ariadne walked gingerly over the muddy bank. It was bad enough when it squished through her toes, but it was even worse when there was a hard nubbin that could be anything. A beetle. A piece of a beer bottle. Part of a dead animal. She shuddered.

"That mud is so gross," she said when she finally reached the grassy area where her parents were setting out the picnic lunch. The dark green trees, already starting to get fall-brown, looked odd growing so near the water, and it was strange to feel cool grass underfoot instead of hot sand. She took a handful of chips.

"Hey, stop that," her father said. "Wait until everyone gets a shot at the food before you eat it all up, Addy. And if the mud bothers you, wear your water shoes."

"Whoever heard of swimming in shoes?" Ariadne grumbled. "If we were still in Florida, we'd have nice clean sand instead of this goo. And we'd have salt water to keep us afloat. And we'd have Sarah down the street."

"And we'd have a mountain of bills," her mother said, "and we wouldn't have a beautiful lake to go swimming in or lots of new kids to meet once school starts next week. Count your blessings."

I can't count that low, thought Ariadne, but she kept her mouth shut.

"Tell Hector it's lunchtime," her father said, and this time Ariadne put on her water shoes before going down to the edge of the lake.

"Heck!" she called. "Come eat!" And she turned back without waiting to find out if he had heard. If he hadn't, there would be more for her. Lately, she couldn't eat enough at one sitting to keep from feeling starved before the next meal.

But by the sound of splashing behind her, he had heard and was heading in. He caught up with her at the picnic blanket and dried off with one of their Florida beach towels, the one with the blue seahorse on it that had always been his special favorite. He seemed to have forgotten the beach, though, and was talking about the lake. The dirty, brown lake with no surf and no dolphins.

"Did you know that if you hold real still, little fishes come up and nibble you all over?" he asked.

"Yeah, I knew that already," said Ariadne. "It's gross."

"It's not gross, it's *cool!*" Hector said. "They wiggle around and look like puppies wagging their tails. I wonder what they're eating off your skin?"

"Salt, I suppose," their mother said.

"See?" said Ariadne. "Even the fish know that salt water is better. I wonder who picked *them* up out of the ocean and dumped them here in this stinky lake."

"Oh, stop complaining," Hector said. "The lake doesn't stink. It smells like a lake is supposed to smell, just like Zephyr smells like a dog is supposed to smell."

"Zephyr stinks," Ariadne said.

"Enough of that, Ariadne Louise," her father broke in. "Quit grousing and say something nice."

Ariadne thought as she chewed and swallowed. "Good deviled eggs," she said finally. "You used the same kind of mayo that we had at home."

Her mother groaned and flopped onto her back on the blanket. "This *is* home for now, my precious. If the college hadn't offered me a job, we might have wound up in Nebraska, or South Dakota, or someplace even farther from home—" She stopped as Ariadne grinned at her. "All right, you caught me. Even farther from *Florida* than where we are right now. Tennessee is pretty close, and Sarah's coming for Thanksgiving. That is, if you still want her. You'll probably have tons of new friends by then and won't want to see her."

"Oh, sure," Ariadne said. Not want to see Sarah? Her best friend since preschool, who'd spent the night so many times that she had her own toothbrush and sleeping bag at Ariadne's house? Really.

"You never know," Hector said. "Sarah might have a new best friend by then."

"She will not!" Ariadne said. "Sarah and I will always be best friends, and even if I have to spend the next six years here, we'll be roommates in college and get jobs together after we graduate."

"Oh, really?" her father said. "And where are you planning on going to college?"

"Florida State," said Ariadne, and when the others laughed, she threw her cookie in the mud and stomped off into the bushes. They were so thick that within seconds she was out of sight of the lake and of her family.

Honestly, she thought. If they liked it so much, they could stay. But she wouldn't. She would e-mail Sarah and beg her to ask her parents once more if Ariadne could move in with them, at least for the rest of middle school. They were finally going to be seventh-graders. They'd have lockers and get to take Spanish or German or French and go to the seventh-grade dance at Halloween. And they were going to be in the same homeroom this year, with Mr. McGerr. Just my luck to get the coolest teacher in the school and then have to leave, she thought as she blinked back tears. This *stinks.*

Why anyone would want to live someplace where they would cover whole towns with water just to make a stupid lake was beyond her. Her father had explained that the dam generated electricity for the entire region and was powered by the water in Cedar Point Lake, but the idea still gave her the creeps. It was like the story her mother had told her about Atlantis, that Greek island-city that sank into the ocean, taking a whole civilization with it. Not that Dobbin, Tennessee, probably had much civilization to lose, but still, a town was under them whenever they went swimming, under the jet-skis—even under those little brown fish. Yuck, there was probably a cemetery under the water too, and who knew what the fish had been dining on before their little mouths nibbled on her?

Ariadne had gone deep into the underbrush, pulling herself up the steep slope by holding on to bushes and small trees. There was nothing to worry about here, no matter how far she strayed. There weren't any Florida alligators, and there was no chance of getting lost when all she had to do was head back downhill to find herself at the lake again.

So why did it feel creepy? Maybe because it was suddenly so still. She realized that she didn't hear any birds, and the rustle of squirrels or possums or whatever it was had stopped abruptly. She was about to turn back when she saw something that made her jump.

Peering out from behind a tree was a girl of about her age. Her pale brown hair was pulled back into a long braid that flopped over one shoulder as she leaned in Ariadne's direction. She wore a faded blue dress and sturdy brown boots. What dorky clothes, thought Ariadne. But maybe that's what kids here wear on their summer vacation.

The girl didn't say anything. She looked at Ariadne without expression. Why didn't the girl speak?

Ariadne shivered. It was cool in the shade, and her hair was still wet.

"Hello," Ariadne said. No answer. "Um—I was just taking a walk. Is this your property?" Still nothing. She took a step toward the girl and stumbled on a fallen branch. She caught her balance and looked back to the tree, but no one was there.

The girl had vanished.

Two

The next afternoon Ariadne was lying on her stomach in her room, channel-surfing. Thank goodness the people they were renting from managed to get cable out here in the boonies, and thank goodness her parents had agreed to keep paying for it. She had to admit that this house was pretty nice, and not just because she'd gotten her own TV. There was also a big screened-in porch, and her cozy room had both a slanted ceiling and a skylight.

Someone knocked at the front door, and Zephyr instantly started barking. She heard the screen door creak, and then her mother said something inaudible. Ariadne hadn't heard a car drive up, so it must be one of the neighbors. The Parrishes next door were friendly, despite what she had heard about country people keeping to themselves. They had even taken Hector out on their jet-ski, and he hadn't shut up about it since.

"Ariadne!" her mother called up the stairs. "It's for you!"

For her? But she didn't know anybody here.

"Who is it?" she called back, pressing the mute button.

"Come down and see," her mother answered.

The screen door squeaked again as she pushed it open. Three girls about her age were sitting on bikes in the front yard. One of them was patting Zephyr, who was wagging his whole fat body along with his tail. Unlike the girl she had seen at the lake, they all wore normal clothes: shorts, T-shirts, beat-up running shoes. They had on bike helmets, and one was wearing a mini-backpack.

"You want to go to town and get some ice cream?" one of them asked. Ariadne looked back at her mother, standing on the porch. She nodded encouragingly.

"Okay," she said. "Just let me get my bike and some money."

The girl with the backpack said, "You don't need any money—my mom gave me enough for all of us," and Ariadne thought, That's why you're asking me; your mom bribed you to invite the new girl when you went to get ice cream.

But she didn't say anything, just got her bike. As she fastened the strap of her helmet, she asked, "Which way is town?"

"Uphill," said the girl with the money. "But that means on the way home we get to coast the whole way." And they took off. Zephyr followed them for a little while, then turned back.

Ariadne, accustomed to biking where a rise of ten feet was considered a big hill, was worn out by the time they pulled up in front of a small ice-cream parlor on the town square. It was squeezed between a diner and a dusty-looking general store. There was a small park across the narrow street, and on the opposite side of it stood a gas station and two churches. On the third edge of the park were a small office building and a white house with a sign saying DOBBIN PUBLIC LIBRARY over the door. On the fourth side was a cemetery filled with small headstones.

The girls propped their bikes against the big glass window with FENDER'S ICE CREAM lettered across the front without bothering to lock them (Ariadne noticed that they didn't even have bike locks) and went in. She stood back while the others debated the flavors, and when it was her turn ordered a double scoop of Rocky Road in a sugar cone.

The gray-haired woman working behind the counter looked sour as she slapped ice cream into the cones. Her glance met Ariadne's when she handed the Rocky Road cone over the counter. Her flat blue eyes were expressionless.

Ariadne followed the girls out the door, and together they walked across the street to the little park. Two of the girls perched on a picnic table while the third sat on the bench. Wordlessly, Ariadne took a seat on the bench too. With her helmet off, the girl next to her turned out to be a freckled redhead, like one of the girls sitting on the table.

The third, who had brought the money, was a blonde, with a pug nose and a wide mouth.

"My mom said you just moved here from Florida," said the blonde. Ariadne nodded, concentrating on catching a drip. The girl groaned and said, "You're so lucky! I've just been to Florida once and I was only three so I don't remember it. But next year—" the taller of the two redheads joined in, "—eighth-grade trip to Disney World!" And they gave each other high fives.

"I bet you know Disney World like we know this town," said the shorter redhead enviously.

"Actually, I've never been," Ariadne said. These were her first words to the girls since they had left the house, and her own voice sounded loud to her.

"You're *kidding!*" said the blonde. "If I lived in Florida, I'd be there every weekend!"

"We didn't live too close to it," Ariadne said, "and every time we planned to go, something would come up."

The others nodded. "Just like parents to get you all excited about something and then discover they're too busy," the taller redhead said. "I'm Ashley, by the way, and we're in the same class next year."

"How do you know whose class I'm going to be in?" Ariadne asked.

"There's only one seventh grade at Polk Middle School," Ashley explained. "I saw your name on the list, but I don't know how to say it."

"A-ree-AD-nee," she answered. "And my brother is named Hector. He's going to Dobbin Elementary."

"Ooh, he could be your new boyfriend, Jessica," Ashley said.

"Shut up," the other redhead said, but without anger, as though she were used to being teased by her sister.

"And I'm Caroline Kennedy," said the blonde. "No relation to the famous one. I'll be in seventh grade too. Where did you get those names from?"

Jessica, Ashley, and Caroline—nice, normal names, thought Ariadne as she launched into the explanation of where she and Hector got their names from for the millionth time.

"My mother's a professor of classical studies," she said. "You know, like Greek and Latin?" The others nodded. "So she named us after characters from Greek myths. It could have been worse. She wanted to name me Penelope, but my father said everybody would call me Cantaloupe, so she changed it to Ariadne."

"Is your dad a professor too?" Caroline asked.

"No," Ariadne said. "He's trying to write screenplays for movies. I mean, he's writing them, and trying to sell them to Hollywood."

"My mom's at the college," Caroline said. "She works in the bookstore."

"And our dad teaches botany," Jessica said.

Ariadne swallowed the little point of her cone and said, "Is the ice-cream lady always that grumpy?"

"Oh, that's Mrs. Harrison. She's usually much worse!" Caroline said. "At least she didn't fuss at us today. Sometimes she yells that we're letting out the air-conditioning, or that we touched the glass over the ice cream and got it smudgy."

"Or that we're taking too long to make up our minds, or that we tracked in mud," Ashley chimed in. "She's *really* cranky."

"And she's crazy," Jessica said.

"Crazy?" Ariadne said.

"Yup," said Ashley. "She sees things."

Since they were sitting in broad daylight in the middle of an ordinary town, it wasn't too scary to be talking about a crazy lady who had just sold them ice cream. At least it wasn't the kind of crazy that meant Mrs. Harrison came after people with a chainsaw, or anything. As long as there was nothing wrong with the ice cream, but the others had obviously eaten lots of cones there and didn't seem worried.

"What kind of things does she see?" Ariadne asked.

"She doesn't talk about it," Caroline said, "and anyway I think she's over it. I heard she saw things when she was younger but doesn't anymore."

"Has she always lived here?" Ariadne asked.

"Almost," said Caroline, who seemed to be the expert. "She lived in the valley until they flooded it, and then she moved up here to town. When she got married, she moved away and came back after she got divorced and her parents died. My grandmother says her parents were just like her—cranky."

"Were they crazy too?" Ariadne asked.

"Not that I ever heard," Caroline said.

"But what kind of things did she see?" Ariadne persisted.

Caroline said, "My grandma says that when Mrs. Harrison was our age, she said she saw people in the woods when there wasn't anybody there. My grandma should know. They went to school together after the dam was built and the kids in the valley had to come up here on the ridge."

"And she talks to herself all the time," Jessica said. "She's always mumbling, even when there are people in there getting ice cream."

"But my grandma said that when Mrs. Harrison was young and saw people in the woods, she would really talk out loud, only with just her half of the conversation," Caroline said.

"Probably just trying to get attention," Jessica said.

"Or crazy," said Ashley.

Three

"Kids, it's time to go!" Ariadne's father called up the stairs. Hector went thudding down, but Ariadne didn't move. She had stayed up late the night before, and had been woken early by jet-skis on the lake. Now, after lunch, she just wanted to stay home and watch TV.

"Ariadne!" her mother called, an edge to her voice. "Get down here right now!"

"I'm coming, I'm coming!" she shouted, her tone echoing her mother's. Fine, she thought as she thumped down the stairs. If they want me to go so badly, I'll go. But the next time we do something, it has to be something *I* want to do. A Humanities Department reception for new faculty did not sound like the most fascinating way to spend an afternoon.

Hector, on the other hand, was excited. Their mother had told him that one of the English professors had a ten-year-old who would be coming. "Ariadne met those girls the other day," he said as they turned off the gravel road onto the paved county road, "but so far I haven't seen a single boy my age in this whole town. I need to meet some-one before school starts."

"Those girls weren't my type," Ariadne said as they reached the paved road.

"And just what is your type?" her father asked from the front seat.

"Sarah," Ariadne and Hector said simultaneously, and Ariadne leaned over and smacked Hector's arm when he burst out laughing.

"Anyway, I met another girl here before those three, and she *definitely* wasn't my type," Ariadne went on, and then instantly regretted it, because of course her mother asked eagerly, "Really? You met another girl? Who?"

"Just some girl at the lake," Ariadne said.

"When?"

"When we had that picnic at the lake and I went for a walk," Ariadne said. "She wore a long dress and weird shoes, and she had a braid. She seemed shy."

"Probably a Mennonite," her father said.

"What's a Mennonite?" Hector asked. "Some kind of alien?"

"Don't be silly," said their father. "They are people who live around here who keep to old ways of doing things. They dress in old-fashioned clothes, and I don't think they drive cars or have electricity in their houses."

"That's Amish," their mother said.

"Mennonite too, I think," said their father.

"Whatever she was, I didn't like her," Ariadne said.

Her mother sighed. "Ariadne, you're in such a stinker of a mood, I wish you had just stayed home," she said.

"Fine," Ariadne said. "Let me out, and I'll walk back."

"Oh, come on," her mother said. "You'll have to meet these people sometime, anyway."

"Why?" Ariadne asked.

Her mother didn't answer, but made an exasperated noise and looked out the window.

"Why? I said," Ariadne demanded. "I don't see why I ever have to meet them."

"All right," her mother said. "I give up. Get out. Walk home."

Silently, her father pulled over to the side of the road, and Ariadne got out. She slammed the door. Her mother rolled down the window and said, "And don't go any-where—stay home until your mood improves."

"Which it won't until I go back to Florida," Ariadne muttered, but not loud enough for anyone to hear.

The car drove away, kicking up dust as it went. She turned back the way they had come. The going was easy enough at first on the asphalt, but after a while she came back to the dirt road. She walked on the edge, where the grass was easier on her sandaled feet than the sharp rocks.

They had driven farther than she thought, and her feet were starting to hurt. Her throat dry. There was no way she was going to walk all the way back without a rest. And if there was some way she could get a drink, that would be even better. It was so hot! She had heard that people around here could knock on someone's door—a total stranger's—and be invited in to sit and have some lemonade or iced tea. But Ariadne wasn't from around here, and she wasn't about to start acting as though she was.

A trail opened off the road to her right. It was probably a shortcut to the lake. She figured she could follow it a little way out of the sun and maybe find a fallen tree to sit on. Then, when she had rested some, she would head back to the house.

She pushed branches out of her way, tripped over vines, and got snagged on pricker bushes. But she pushed on, and after a few minutes she found herself at the edge of the lake. The water looked so cool that she wished her father hadn't warned her against drinking it. "Don't ever drink downstream of cows, Addy," he had said, and laughed at the grossed-out face she made when she realized why.

But at least she could cool her feet and get the road dust out from between her toes. That flat rock in the shade of the big old tree would be perfect to sit on. She eased her sandals off, noticing the blister that had started to form on her left heel. She sat down, her feet dangling in the water.

It was so quiet, with no one telling her what to do or teasing her about missing Florida, or trying to convince her that once school started she would make new friends who would become as important to her as Sarah. She impatiently brushed away the tears that suddenly stung her eyes.

Those girls the other day had been nice, but they didn't know anything about her, and she didn't know anything about them. She had been at Sarah's house when Sarah lost her first tooth, and Sarah had sat in the emergency room with her when she had her chin stitched up after she had tripped over Zephyr when he was a new puppy. Sarah had even been the one to name Zephyr, in a way. Sarah and Ariadne were only four when Ariadne's dad brought him home, and both girls still loved Peter Pan. Sarah had named her cat Peter and wanted Ariadne to call her new Labrador Wendy.

"You can't," Ariadne's father had said. "Wendy is a girl's name, and this is a boy dog."

"Well, the god of the west wind is Zephyr," her mother had said, "and if we name him Zephyr, it will be kind of like calling him Windy." Her father had laughed, and so the dog was named. Ariadne scowled at the memory. I wonder if that's how they thought of my name, she thought. Making some dumb joke.

She stretched out on her back, resting on the soft moss that covered most of the rock. It sure was comfortable here. The waves made a tiny splashing sound, and the shade was nice and cool. She closed her eyes and thought about the time the two of them had drawn freckles all over her nose to match Sarah's, and how they were about to dye Sarah's hair black when Ariadne's mother had caught them.

That last memory was enough to convince her. She and Sarah belonged together, and Ariadne belonged at her old school with all her old friends, and her parents had been cruel to bring her here. She would just have to go back. She would get all her money out of her drawer and ride her bike to the nearest bus station. She would buy a bus ticket and get as close to her old house as she could, and then she would call Sarah. Sarah's mom would have to pick her up, and then her parents would see that she meant it, that she didn't want to live in Tennessee on a muddy lake with a drowned town under it.

When she opened her eyes again, she realized that she must have fallen asleep. The shade cast by the tree overhead extended over the water now. And she was just dying of thirst. Cow poop or no cow poop, if she didn't get home soon, she was going to take a drink out of that lake. She sat up and strapped on her sandals. And froze. There, half-hidden by the bush next to her, was that same girl, the silent one, wearing the same faded blue dress and the brown boots that went halfway up her ankles. Ariadne caught a glint of something around her neck.

"Hey," Ariadne said. The girl ducked her head a little but did not reply.

Ariadne's thirst burned even hotter. She licked her dry lips. Maybe the girl could get her a drink.

"Do you live near here?" The girl jerked her head back over her shoulder as if indicating a place.

"Do you think I could get a drink of water there?" Ariadne asked.

"No," the girl finally said. She had a quiet, almost thin voice. "There's no water there. The well ran dry." She spoke with the soft accent of the country people Ariadne had heard in the stores nearby.

"So where do you get your water from?" Ariadne asked. The girl shrugged and looked away, back into the woods.

"Well, if I can't get any water from you, I'd better be getting home," said Ariadne, exasperated and ready to kill for a drink. The girl didn't answer. Ariadne hadn't really expected her to. She got to her feet and ducked under a branch, heading up the hill. She suddenly felt as though the index finger on her left hand were on fire.

"Yeeow!" she yelled, and clapping her hand in her armpit, she danced up and down, shrieking, "Ow! Damn it!" She must have brushed against a bee as she pushed back the bushes.

Suddenly the other girl was next to her. "You don't want to do that," she said, and pulled at Ariadne's arm with surprising strength. Her suntanned hand was dry and cool as she gently straightened Ariadne's finger. "The stinger's still in there." The other girl frowned and scratched against the stinger with her fingernail until it popped out. Ariadne was so surprised that she made no attempt to resist, despite the sharp pain as the fingernail scraped the sore spot. There was something gentle in the girl's touch that soothed the heat of the sting and made Ariadne's finger feel cool and almost pleasantly numb. It must be the relief of getting that sharp little thing out of her finger.

"Here, now you need to cool it off," the girl said, and led Ariadne down to the water's edge. The girl continued to hold Ariadne's finger straight out while she scooped up some mud from the edge of the water with her free hand. She slapped it onto the fiery red fingertip. She was intent on her work, and her brow was still furrowed. Now Ariadne could see that the glint at her neck was a locket on a gold chain.

"Does it feel better?" she asked, and Ariadne nodded. The cool mud was really making a difference. When the girl let go of her hand, Ariadne sat back down on her flat rock and waited as the throbbing in her finger faded a little.

"Why didn't you talk to me before?" she asked.

"You didn't need me before," the girl replied.

"Do you only talk when people need you?" Ariadne asked. The girl shrugged, then looked away into the distance again.

"What's your name?" Ariadne asked.

"May," said the girl, still looking into the woods. "May Butler."

"I'm Ariadne Fellowes," Ariadne said. There was no reply. It was Ariadne's turn to shrug. Her mudpack was warming up again, and although there was less pain in her finger, it was by no means gone, so she scooped up another handful of cold mud. She formed it into a neat ball around her finger and laughed. She held it up.

"Look, May!" she said. "E.T. phone home!"

But once again, May had silently gone.

four

Hector and his new friend, Bruce, were going fishing with Bruce's father. Ariadne's father was at a tricky spot in a screenplay, and her mother had to go to the college to plan some course work. So Ariadne was left on her own.

"Why don't you find those girls you had ice cream with?" her father asked the third time she interrupted him. She shook her head. "Well, bake some cookies or something," he said. But they were out of flour. Going for a bike ride was better than nothing, she finally decided. She didn't have anywhere in particular to go, so she rode toward town.

The houses were far apart from each other, and there was no sidewalk. There was barely even a road until their street joined the paved county road a few miles away. As she passed a big white house with a screened-in porch like hers, she heard someone call her name. She skidded in the dust as she put on the brakes, and looked around.

"Ariadne!" she heard again. "Over here!" and a hand waved out an upstairs window. She shaded her eyes against the sun, and there at the window was Caroline, the blond girl from the other day.

"Where you going?" she called down.

"Nowhere," Ariadne said. "Just riding around."

"Well, come on up," said Caroline, and she disappeared before Ariadne could answer. Ariadne wheeled her bike to the house. She stood at the screen door, feeling foolish. No one came to let her in, and there was no doorbell. So what was she supposed to do? She tried the door and found it open. Cautiously, she poked her head in. "Hello?" she called, and when there was no answer, she took a step inside. "Hello?" she called again, and the most beautiful girl she had ever seen stepped through a door. Blond hair hung almost to her waist, and her pale face set off enormous eyes the color of emeralds.

"What?" she said, looking around, and then, seeing Ariadne, "Oh, are you a friend of the dork's?" Taking this to mean Caroline, Ariadne nodded, and the girl said, "She's in her room. You can go up if you don't get nauseous too easily." And she disappeared.

Ariadne walked up the stairs, expecting at every step that some parent would come out and demand to know who she was and who gave her permission to wander around this house. Back home nobody would leave a door unlocked, and nobody would let a perfect stranger into the house like this. But she didn't see anyone. When she reached the top of the stairs, she heard music coming from one of the rooms. She knocked. The door opened and Caroline, waving her left hand to dry the nail polish, motioned her in.

"Hey, what took you so long?" she asked, and then, without waiting for an answer, said, "Do you like this color?"

The polish on Caroline's chewed-up nails was deep purple, and Ariadne didn't particularly care for it, but she nodded and said, "Cool." She settled down on the bed next to Caroline and watched her do the manicure.

"Yeah, it's pretty nice, isn't it?" said Caroline, extending her fingers and looking at the nails with satisfaction. Then she started painting the other hand.

"Who was that girl downstairs?" Ariadne asked.

"Girl? Oh, Jade. My sister. She's going to be a senior this year. She's a royal pain."

"She's gorgeous," Ariadne said.

Caroline nodded without looking up. "I know," she said. "Gives me hope. You should have seen her at our age. What an absolute dog! Course, she was sick, but she looked like a mess even before she got sick. And if she can get that beautiful, maybe I'll look human someday." Caroline wasn't exactly homely, but she did seem like an ugly duckling next to that swan downstairs.

"What was she sick with?"

"Leukemia." Caroline held up her right hand and blew on the nails. "She was supposed to die. She got all skinny, and her hair got nasty, and she threw up all the time, but they used some experimental medicine on her and it worked, because not only is she supposedly in one hundred percent remission, but her hair grew back and she isn't what you'd exactly call skinny anymore."

"No, she isn't," Ariadne agreed, remembering the older girl's curves.

"She wants to be a model, so she changed her name to Jade and had pictures made last spring. My parents had a fit and threw them out and said that after she finishes high school they'll discuss it."

"It must have been scary having her be so sick," Ariadne said, and Caroline nodded, waving both hands in the air.

"It was," she said. "I was only seven, and for some reason I really liked her then. She used to come to my room and cry that I was going to grow up and she wasn't, and it wasn't fair. It made me feel guilty, and I told her I didn't want to talk about it. That got her so mad that she went and invented a better sister or best friend or something. Weird, isn't it?" Ariadne nodded. "I mean, there she was, twelve years old, with an imaginary friend. She got mad if you said her friend didn't exist. She said her friend was a good listener. The opposite of me, I suppose. Once I

followed her and heard her talking, only there wasn't anyone there."

"She must have been really scared to act so weird."

"That's what my parents kept saying. Anyway, after
her last stay at the hospital in Nashville, she didn't talk
about her imaginary friend anymore, and then she got
better. And then she got beautiful."

Ariadne watched Caroline paint her toenails. When
they were all purple, she stood up and said, "Well, I guess
I'd better be going."

Caroline looked up in surprise. "But I thought you said
you weren't on your way to anywhere."

"I'm not," Ariadne said, "I mean, I wasn't. I just don't
want to bother you—"

"You're not bothering me," Caroline said. "This is
mostly what we do in the summer, anyway, just hang out
and talk. We can't have jobs until we're old enough to
drive, and after a while the lake gets really boring."

Ariadne could relate to that, but she knew she shouldn't
agree out loud. After all, it wasn't as though it was her lake
to criticize. "So what do you want to do?" she asked.

Caroline said, "Ice cream?" and Ariadne agreed.

As they leaned their bikes against the storefront,
Ariadne suddenly felt uncomfortable. She didn't want

to go in and face that cranky woman again. "I know what," she said. "Let's go to the diner and get some fries instead."

Caroline shrugged. "Sure. And we can get a discount if Jade's boyfriend is working today. He's much too nice for her."

But they were out of luck and had to pay full price. They got the fries to go and took them to the little dusty park where they had eaten their ice cream the other day.

"So you're not too crazy about Cedar Point Lake?" Ariadne began cautiously.

"It's okay," Caroline said. "It's just that it's not that big, and it's never very exciting. It must have been really exciting when they made it, though. Imagine all that water covering up the whole valley!"

"My dad said it was made by a dam, and there was a town under there before," Ariadne said.

"Not what you'd call a town," Caroline said. "Every year they have a reunion of the people who used to live in the hollow, and only about five of them show up, and they talk about what a great place it was." She shook her head. "It was more like a few farms and that kind of thing, not a real town."

"Was there a cemetery?" Ariadne asked.

"There was one by the church down there, but they unburied everyone or whatever you call it—"

"Disinterred," Ariadne murmured, and then bit her tongue, ashamed for showing off. But it didn't seem to bother Caroline.

"Disinterred, right. And they reburied them in our cemetery up here. But they probably didn't get all the bones, because some families had private graveyards behind their houses—some still do. I know," she said as Ariadne made a face. "Can you imagine riding your bike over your grandfather? And when they moved the bones, they got jumbled up, so they just made one big tombstone with all the names on it. Want to see?"

"Sure," Ariadne said, to be polite. Still eating their fries, the two girls walked through the square.

"Our bikes!" Ariadne said.

"Oh, that's all right," Caroline said. "We don't have to go far."

"But won't someone take them?" Ariadne asked.

"Who would want two beat-up bikes?" Caroline asked.

Lots of tombstones crowded the little cemetery, some in rows, but some just scattered around. The ones with older dates tilted at odd angles. They were hard to read, being black and mossy, and a few of them just had a name, no date or Bible verse or anything.

"Those are people that lived in Dobbin. Ridge-runners," Caroline said proudly, as though this were a title of honor. "That means people who lived on top of the hill, like my grandparents. Here's the stone for the people in the valley," and she pointed down at a flat pinkish stone inscribed with a few dozen names. Ariadne bent over.

"They made it flat so it would be easier to cut the grass around it," Caroline said, but Ariadne didn't answer. She was looking at the names, going back to the late 1700s.

"Look," she said, "there's a bunch of Fenders."

Caroline bent over to see. "That's cranky Mrs. Harrison's family. My grandma said that they used to live in the valley and had to move up here when it got flooded. That must be when Mrs. Harrison went nuts."

But Ariadne wasn't listening. She had caught sight of a long string of Butlers, starting in the 1700s. But they dwindled in the late 1800s. There wasn't a single Butler with a birth date past 1880.

five

That was odd, though maybe she hadn't heard May's last name right. Or maybe her family had moved here after the dam was built. But she talked like the country people around here, and there was something that Ariadne couldn't put her finger on that made her look like she belonged here. And she sure was familiar with the woods, the way she kept disappearing so fast.

Ariadne didn't say anything as they rode toward Caroline's house. It was nice to have the downhill stretch on their way home. They went side by side, coasting and then braking when they started going too fast.

"I think I have all my school supplies," Caroline said, "at least until they tell us what else we need to get. But I still need to figure out what I'm wearing tomorrow. What are you wearing?"

"I thought these shorts and a green T-shirt," Ariadne said. "What about you?"

"Something like that," she said. "We're not very formal at Polk Middle."

I bet you're not, thought Ariadne. And I bet it's a one-room schoolhouse with a bell outside that the teacher rings when recess is over. She wished for the thousandth time that she was back home, with the computer lab and the science room with all its shiny equipment just waiting for seventh-grade hands to get to work on them.

"I bet our middle school will seem really small and backward after what you're used to," Caroline said, as though reading her mind. "You probably have all sorts of things that we don't." Ariadne shrugged. She didn't want to agree too eagerly.

"How many kids were in your grade at your old school?" Caroline asked. Ariadne pictured the way the seventh-grade corridor had looked on the last day of school. She and Sarah and their other friends had taken a walk down it, imagining themselves there the next year. The PTA had raised a lot of money to update the computer lab, and all the computers had Internet connections. Here the most recent technology would probably be a light-up globe.

And most of the kids had probably known each other forever and would never accept someone new who came in seventh grade. Jeffy Bigelow had told her about things his brother said people did to new kids in middle school—locking you in lockers, stuffing you in trash cans, giving you swirlies, which Jeffy explained meant sticking your head in the toilet and flushing it.

These sounded more like things boys would do to each other, but Ariadne knew that girls could remind you that you weren't really one of them too. Like not talking to you, or playing tricks on you to make you feel like an outsider.

Caroline was looking at her in a funny way, and Ariadne realized she hadn't answered her question yet.

"Let's see, there are four classrooms, and each one has about twenty-five or thirty kids in it," she began.

"So, that's what—more than one hundred kids? Just in the seventh grade?" Caroline asked. "That's bigger than our whole middle school!"

"The high school's even bigger," Ariadne said.

"Jeez. We only have about twenty in each grade. How do you get to know everybody?"

"Oh, I've known most of them since kindergarten," Ariadne said.

"I have a lot of friends from that long ago too," Caroline said. "And some whose parents went to school with my parents. And there are even some of the same teachers at Polk that my parents had. The seventh-grade teacher is new, though. My mom said she's nice, but I'm going to judge for myself. She's probably an ogre, but my mom thinks that if she says she's nice, I'll go in with a positive attitude."

"So have you known everybody there since you were little?"

"Some," Caroline said. "Libby Walker is great; she is so funny you could die. Let's see—Katie French is nice, but she's really quiet. Then there's Susan White, but I'd just as soon not have known her for a week, much less my whole life."

"That bad?" Ariadne asked.

"The worst," Caroline said. "Not to mention Sam Hagerman. He is just so disgusting, and the more you know him, the worse he is." He sounded like Jeffy Bigelow back home.

They had reached Caroline's house and were wheeling their bikes up onto the porch.

"Have you known Ashley and Jessica forever?" Ariadne asked.

"No, they just came two years ago," Caroline said. "You're not going to be the only new one. Lots of the college professors live around here, and they come and go pretty fast."

"So you know everyone who lives here?" Ariadne asked.

"Sure do," Caroline said. "As long as they've been here a little while, that is. Why, did you meet someone that you want to know about? Go ahead. Ask me anything." And she sat down on the porch glider and assumed a pose like a mystic, legs crossed, eyes closed, hands dramatically on her forehead as though concentrating.

"Do you know a little kid named Bruce?"

Caroline opened her eyes and made a face. "You mean that dweeb with the hair that sticks straight up?"

Ariadne nodded.

"He's a little toad. How do you know him?"

"He's my brother's new friend. He's always over at our house now, or Hector's at his."

Caroline groaned. "Lucky you. Just don't let him follow you over here, okay?"

"Okay," Ariadne said, pleased that Caroline assumed she'd be coming over again.

"Try me on another one," Caroline said.

"May," Ariadne said.

"Who?"

"May Butler."

"I don't know any Butlers, and I never heard of anyone called May. Sounds like an old-fashioned name," Caroline said. "Must be new. Is she going into seventh grade?"

"I don't know," Ariadne said. "She doesn't talk much. But she seemed about our age, and I think she's from around here."

"Where did you meet her?"

"Down by the lake one day," Ariadne said. "And then yesterday in the woods. She talked like she was from here, and she sure seems familiar with the woods. If you take your eyes off her for a second, she's gone."

"New one on me," Caroline said. "Maybe she's home-schooled. I wonder if Jade-green knows who she is. She might have a big brother that Jade has flirted with, like all the other boys at the high school."

"Oh, it doesn't matter," Ariadne said, but Caroline went into the house and called, "Jade!" Ariadne followed her tentatively. There was no answer. Caroline poked her head in the door where the gorgeous blonde had appeared before. "Jade!" she called louder.

"What do you want?"

"Do you know anybody named May Butler?"

Silence.

"Jade! Do you know a Butler family around here?"

"Who wants to know?"

"My friend Ariadne." Caroline grinned over her shoulder at Ariadne. She grinned back, pleased at being called a friend.

Again silence. Then, "Tell your friend Ariadne to mind her own business," came the voice, and a door slammed.

"Guess not," Caroline said, coming back in. "And aren't you glad you don't have a sister? Did you ever hear anything so rude?"

But Ariadne had heard something more than rudeness. She had heard fear, and the fear in the older girl's voice made the back of her own neck prickle.

Six

Ariadne groaned, looking at the pile of clothes on her bed. The first day, the new kids would be pegged as to what kind of person they were, based mostly on what they wore. At home she could call Sarah, and they could arrange to be dressed similarly—not identically, since that would be just too weird, but close enough. Here she was going to have to run the risk of looking totally different.

Her mother came into the room. "I just talked to Stacy Jarman," she said. "She teaches in my department and has two girls, an eighth-grader and a sixth-grader. Stacy tells me that they're planning to wear denim shorts, T-shirts, sneakers—"

"Running shoes," interrupted Ariadne.

"Whatever," her mother said. "Their mom said sneakers, but she's probably as ancient as I am and doesn't know the right word either. So that gives you some idea. Okay?"

"Okay," Ariadne said. "Thanks for asking your friend, Mom."

Her mother made a Groucho face and wiggled an imaginary cigar at her. "All in a day's woik, little lady," she said. "If you do the laundry tonight, the shorts will be clean for tomorrow, although why it has to be those particular shorts and not any others, I don't know. And you must have some other T-shirt that would suit you."

So that was settled. Ariadne turned on the computer and, while she waited for it to boot up, thought about what she would write to Sarah. Not much else had happened since yesterday. Maybe she'd tell Sarah how afraid she was to be the new kid when all her life she had been surrounded by people she had always known. It seemed so wrong, somehow, because Ariadne was always the one teachers asked to make the new kid feel welcome. She'd say how uncomfortable it was going to feel to be on the receiving end of someone else's kindness, not the giving end. And how much she missed her, and couldn't wait until Thanksgiving.

Great—she had mail. It had to be from Sarah. It was. And Sarah had already had her first day of school.

hey
in first period jeffy bigelow sat next to me and asked
me where you were. i said you moved to tn and he told
me to ask you if youve quit wearing shoes and if you
were calling hector bubba. i told him to shut up and

mr mcgerr heard me and didnt get mad at me for saying shut up, just wanted to know what we were talking about. hes so cool!!!! i told him we were talking about my friend who moved to tn and so he told us all about his trip to graceland after elvis died. have you been to graceland yet? can we go when i come at thanksgiving?

Ariadne shook her head in exasperation. She kept telling everybody back home that Graceland was hundreds of miles away from Dobbin, but they didn't seem to believe her any more than people here did when she said that Disney World was hundreds of miles away from her home in Florida.

Sarah went on to tell about the science lab and about how Alison Gray was her lab partner and they had already messed up an experiment and how funny it was. Great, Ariadne thought. Alison was just waiting to leap in and take over as Sarah's best friend. She turned off the computer without bothering to reply. She didn't have anything to say until she had some first-day-of-school stories of her own to share. Besides, she didn't feel like it right now.

Suddenly the house felt stuffy. She stepped out the back door, where she could breathe a little better. What was Zephyr doing in the bushes? He was sure making a racket. She followed him down the slope a little way and saw that he had chased a squirrel up a tree. She shooed away the dog and then moved back herself. She sat down on the grass and watched, trying not to move, to see what the squirrel would do.

"It's all right," said a voice from behind her, and she jumped. Before she even turned around, she had a feeling who it was, and sure enough, there was that strange May. The girl hung back, blending in with the trees and their shadows until she was almost invisible.

"What's all right?" Ariadne asked, and then, "Why do you keep sneaking up on me?"

"The squirrel," May said. "It will be all right once the dog is gone. See, it's already down," and Ariadne looked back at the now-empty tree.

"Why do you sneak up on me?" Ariadne asked, but she knew that May would just shrug and look away, which is exactly what she did. Ariadne felt that odd prickle on the back of her neck again. What's there to be afraid of? she asked herself.

"Are you excited about going to school tomorrow?" she asked, trying to get the conversation back to a normal subject again.

May just stood and gazed out through the trees as though she were staring at the lake. She was silent for so long that Ariadne thought she hadn't heard, but then she said, "School tomorrow? Oh no, I don't go to school."

Well, that could explain why Caroline had never heard of her.

"Are you home-schooled?" Ariadne asked.

"I guess."

Silence. Then Ariadne asked, "Did you say your last name was Butler?"

May nodded.

"Did you just move here?"

"Lived here all my life," she said. "Born right in the hollow. So were my momma and daddy. And my daddy's daddy too."

"Then why doesn't anybody know you?"

"Plenty of people know me," she said softly, looking down at her heavy shoes.

"Well, who do you know? Girls our age, I mean. You're about twelve, aren't you?"

May nodded again but cast an uneasy glance over her shoulder. Ariadne followed her gaze. What was she looking for? Those thick shadows could hide anything.

"So who do you know?"

"I know Ann," May said, almost wistfully. "Do you know Ann?"

Ariadne shook her head. "I just moved here," she said. "I haven't met anybody named Ann. But maybe I will at school tomorrow."

"Ann's nice. And Leslie," May said. "I know Leslie. I wish I could see her sometime. She's been sick, so maybe that's why she doesn't come to see me anymore. I hope she's better."

"Leslie?" Ariadne said. "I don't know a Leslie. I know a Caroline, and two sisters named Ashley and Jessica. Do you know them?"

May shook her head. "Ann and Leslie are the only girls I know," she said.

"How do you know them if you didn't meet them at school? Church?"

May shook her head again. She was playing with the end of her long, light-brown braid as though avoiding Ariadne's eye. "I just met them, I guess," she said. "Like I met you."

"Do you ever go to town?" Ariadne asked. "It's not much of a town, but we could get an ice cream."

"Oh no," May said, as though frightened, and she retreated a little farther into the shadows. "I'm not allowed into town."

"Not allowed?" Ariadne asked. "Are you grounded?"

May shook her head, looking bewildered. "I can't go far from home," she said. "I have to stay near in case they need me."

"Why would they need you?"

"I have to go now," May said.

"But why?" Ariadne asked. "Why can't you stay?"

"I just can't," May said. And she fled into the trees so swiftly that Ariadne lost sight of her in an instant.

She pushed down the uneasiness she felt rising in her belly. She had more important things to think of right now than a strange girl. Like school tomorrow. Like Jeffy Bigelow thinking she had turned into a hillbilly. Like Sarah writing her a whole message and not saying even once that she missed her.

seven

"Are you sure you don't want me to drive you?" her father asked once again. "Last chance!"

"No," said Ariadne. "I want to go by myself. I can ride my bike—it's not far, and I'm too old for my daddy to come in and introduce himself to my teacher. Just take Hector."

"Are you sure you can find it?"

"Dad," she said impatiently. "There's only one road. Besides, all I have to do is follow the other kids." Hector, already in the car, was blowing the horn impatiently, and it drove her crazy. "Go on," she said. "I'll leave in a minute."

"Well, all right," he said. "Just go soon. You don't want to be late your first day."

She rolled her eyes. "Leave, Dad! Leave!" she said, pushing him out the door.

He laughed and let himself be pushed. At the car he turned and waved. "Have a good first day, Addy," he called, and she waved back.

Just *go,* she thought, and he finally did.

The house was empty now. Her mother's classes had started, and she was already serving on some committee about trying to get more students to take foreign languages. So these days she left before Ariadne was even up. Every night at dinner she talked about the other people at the college as though she had known them for years. Ariadne wished she was forty instead of twelve. Everything would be a lot easier.

She wasn't sure how long it would take to bike to school, but she knew that it would be disastrous to arrive late on the first day. Imagine walking into a room full of quiet people listening to the teacher and having them all watch as you looked around for a seat and had to sit by yourself. She shuddered and pulled on her helmet, then threw her leg over the bike and took off. If she was too early, she would just pedal more slowly when she got close.

But she had timed it right. There were some bikes in the rack out front, and kids were talking in groups, laughing, calling to each other. She was relieved that most of the others were wearing shorts and T-shirts, and her olive-green shirt seemed just about right: not too bright and not too dull. She tried to look busy as she pushed her bike into the rack.

A bell rang—at least the school bells were the same here, loud and obnoxious and going on forever—and the groups broke up as kids streamed into the building. Now how am I supposed to know where to go? she thought, and for a second wished she had allowed her father to come with her. He would have just walked up to someone and said, "Where does a new seventh-grader go?" but she would die rather than do that.

The first room she looked into gave her a shock. Two rows of gleaming computers, already booted up, sat on metal tables. Each had a separate printer, and from the cables it looked like they were networked. Wow, she thought. Maybe this place isn't as backward as I thought. But the halls were rapidly becoming empty, and she still hadn't found her classroom.

"Can I help you?" She spun around to see a young African-American woman wearing a suit and carrying an armful of books.

"I'm looking for the seventh-grade classroom," she muttered, looking down at her feet.

The woman said, "Come on. I'm going there myself. I'm the seventh-grade teacher, Ms. Saylor."

"Oh," said Ariadne, wishing she could think of something to say.

"You must be new," said Ms. Saylor as they walked down the corridor. Ariadne nodded. "Me too," said Ms. Saylor. "I stayed up half the night wondering what to wear today."

Ariadne said, "You look fine," and hoped she didn't sound too stupid.

"So do you," said the teacher. "Here, why don't you go in first and find a seat so it doesn't look like I walked you to the classroom." Which is exactly what you did, thought Ariadne, but she just said, "Thanks," and let herself in.

Caroline had said there were only about twenty kids in each class, but it sure looked like more than that. Maybe it was because nobody was sitting still, and most of them were making a lot of noise. She looked around and saw Caroline saying something to Ashley that made both of them break into hysterical laughter. Caroline caught sight of Ariadne and waved at her, but then went back to talking to Ashley. There were no empty seats nearby, and anyway, she didn't want to force herself on them when they obviously didn't care if she sat with them or not, so she slid into a chair near the door.

She laid her hands on the desk, but when she moved them she saw that they had left streaks of sweat, so she put them in her lap instead. Now I look just like a sweet little schoolgirl, she thought. Terrific. If she were at home now, she'd be right in the middle of things and would be the first person the teacher would have to tell to sit down and be quiet. No need to tell me that now, she thought, as she sat in silence.

Just then the door opened and Ms. Saylor walked in. Except for her navy-blue suit, she looked like a high-school student. She gave Ariadne a tight smile as she passed her, and Ariadne realized that the teacher was as nervous as she was.

No one paid any attention to Ms. Saylor as she stood at the front of the classroom. She looked like she was about to say something when the intercom buzzed, making her jump. She tried to cover it up, but Ariadne had seen. A boy's voice came crackling into the classroom: "Welcome to Polk Middle School!" The kids burst into a mixture of loud cheers and groans, drowning out what he said after that, and the next words Ariadne could hear were ". . . for the Pledge of Allegiance."

Well, here at least she knew what to do, and like the others she rose to her feet with her hand over her heart and recited the familiar words. *Back home, Sarah's doing the same thing right now,* she thought, and to her horror she felt tears coming to her eyes. She mouthed the end of the pledge, "with liberty and justice for all," without saying them aloud because she was afraid a sob would burst out along with the words.

Then they all sat down. Ms. Saylor cleared her throat. "Good morning!" she said with what sounded like forced cheerfulness. Murmurs of "good morning" came from various spots around the room, and Ms. Saylor plowed on. "I hope this is the seventh-grade classroom, because I'm the seventh-grade teacher," she announced. No one said anything. "I'm going to tell you a little about myself, and then I want all of you to tell me about yourselves too. I know that a lot of you know each other already, but there are some new students," and she smiled at Ariadne, who ducked her head as she felt herself turning red, "who need introducing, and I need to get to know all of you, new and old."

Still no response. The teacher's smile was looking stiff. "My name is Ms. Saylor, and I'm from Chattanooga. I'm glad to be teaching seventh grade because seventh grade was my favorite school year, and I would like to re-create that experience for you. We'll be doing a lot of fun things this year, like using the Internet, doing a social-studies project" (she ignored the groans), "working on a science project that will take us outdoors a lot" (people settled down and started paying attention), "finding pen pals in Spain or Latin America to help us learn Spanish" (more interest), "using math in real-world situations, making a class newspaper, and reading books that you will choose yourself. From a list that I will provide," she added hastily.

She had their attention now. Ariadne looked around and saw that no one was making a face or whispering to a neighbor. Well, at least *she* started off well, she thought.

"Now," said Ms. Saylor, sounding more relaxed, "let's see who all of you are, starting against the wall," and to Ariadne's horror, she pointed to her. Why me? she thought. Why do I have to be the first one? Ms. Saylor nodded encouragingly, and Ariadne forced herself to speak.

"My name—"

But Ms. Saylor interrupted her. "Why don't you stand up so we can all hear you?" Oh, horrors! But she had no choice, so she pushed herself out from behind the little desk and stood over her chair, not knowing where to look.

"My name is Ariadne Fellowes," she said. "I just moved here from Florida. My mother teaches at the college and my dad is a screenwriter. I have a dog named Zephyr." She sat down, then rose to a semi-crouch again. "Oh yeah, and a brother named Hector." Some of the others laughed, and she flushed before she realized that they thought she had been funny on purpose, so she smiled back.

She could hardly pay attention as the others introduced themselves, so relieved was she that her turn was over. But as she listened, wondering how she was ever going to remember all those new names, she noticed that Caroline was right—a few of the others had just moved there too. She also noticed that there was no one named Ann or Leslie in the class. Maybe they're in eighth, thought Ariadne. Or sixth. May hadn't seemed too clear about things at school.

Suddenly the bell rang again. "Since this is a half day, we're making each class period only half as long as it normally will be," said Ms. Saylor. "Next on your schedule is art, and then P.E." Great, thought Ariadne. We get to go someplace else, and when we come back maybe I can find a seat closer to Caroline and Ashley. But as she got up, Ms. Saylor called after the departing class, "For the next few weeks, stay in the same seats you had today, until I get to know your names."

Terrific, she thought. Just terrific. And she got swept up in a group of noisy people and found herself in the art room, and then in the gym, where a teacher went on and on about personal hygiene and how important it was now that they were becoming young ladies.

Then back to the classroom for math and social studies and the rest of it. She wrote her name in her books and looked around, occasionally tuning in to what the teacher was saying. Finally the early dismissal bell came. As they left, Ms. Saylor passed out a sheet of paper with everyone's name and phone number on it. Ariadne was panting with eagerness to escape all that chatter and cheeriness that had nothing to do with her, so she stuffed it in her backpack without even looking at it. Then she pushed her way through the crowd, hopped on her bike, and took off.

At last it was over and she could get out of there. She put her head down and pedaled hard up the little rise outside the school, twinges of embarrassment giving strength to her legs. She thought back over the day, which seemed to go on forever, even though it was only half as long as usual.

Art had been okay, and at least Ashley was at her table, but P.E. was its usual disaster. She couldn't throw anything, she couldn't catch anything, and despite her long legs she couldn't run very fast. Luckily, no one seemed to notice, and when the mercifully shortened class was over, they all went to computer lab, where an eighth-grade student helped them set up their own personal Web pages. That was so cool, she thought. That computer is a lot more powerful than the ones in the lab at home. Wait till I give Sarah my URL.

She had been wrong about the school. It was bright and modern, and the gym was huge and brand-new. But she wasn't wrong about the kids. They didn't know her, and they didn't appear to want to. They just talked and laughed with the people they already knew. Well, she could do without them too.

In a few minutes she had crested the rise at the town square and was on the downhill coasting part, and she leaned back on the bike saddle, keeping just one hand on the brake. Thank goodness, thank goodness, she kept telling herself, and in less than half the time it had taken her to get there that morning, she was home. She jumped off her bike, not even bothering to put down the kickstand, and it clattered onto the flagstones by the door. She ran into the den and stood in the blessed silence and privacy for a few minutes.

Now to the computer. No message from Sarah, but then Sarah had a full day and wouldn't be home yet. So she sat and thought about what she could tell her without sounding too pathetic.

hey

school started today and it was ok. remember that girl
ashley i told you about? i sat next to her in art and shes
really good. they have the coolest computers and i
made a web page. they dont have a science lab but
every week theres a field trip to the college where my
mom teaches and they let us use theirs. so it works out
ok. also theres this room called the virtual learning
project, where you can go if you sign up for a class they
dont have at polk, like german or advanced math or
something, and its like youre in the classroom in some
other school. they have a camera and microphone so
you can ask questions and everything just like you were
there and you see the teacher on a tv. you email your
homework to the teacher and they email it back. so far
they have all the classes i want at polk but im trying to
think of something to take that they dont have so i can
use the vlp. what do you think i should ask for? we had a
half day so i didnt get any lunch and im starved. e you
later!

<3 a

  She logged off and went into the kitchen. She pulled a
bag of chips out of the cupboard, and a jar of salsa and a can
of soda from the refrigerator, and went outside. She sat on
the stone bench under the big mimosa tree behind the
house. Right in front of her, the hill dropped away to the

lake. She leaned back on the bench and stared at the water as she munched on the chips.

She wasn't really surprised when May showed up. The girl seemed to know when she would be outside and alone. Was she spying on her? Or did she just hang out near the lake all the time?

"Want a chip?" she asked, extending the bag, but May shook her head and shrank back a little. She seemed even less talkative than usual. She looked at Ariadne as though waiting for her to say something. But what? The silence stretched out until Ariadne couldn't stand it anymore. Anyway, she needed someone to listen while she talked about that nerve-racking first day, even if it was someone she didn't know at all well.

"That school is awful," she finally said. "You're lucky your parents don't make you go there." Okay, so maybe the school wasn't really awful. But it had been a rotten day.

May didn't say anything, just looked down and twisted the end of her braid. Ariadne swallowed hard past a lump in her throat that wasn't made of chips and salsa.

"It's really small, and there are just about no books in the library," she went on, "and some of the kids seem like real jerks. There's one boy who thinks that it's fun to throw spitballs. I thought that went out in the sixties." May looked puzzled. Jeez, didn't she even know what a spitball was?

"There are lots of girls in seventh grade," Ariadne went on. "But no Ann or Leslie. Are you sure they still live here?"

"No," May said. "I haven't seen either of them for a while. Maybe they moved away. Or maybe they don't need me anymore."

"Need you?" Ariadne said. "What do you mean, need you?"

"They needed someone to talk to," May said. "They didn't have anyone, and my momma told me always to help people in trouble, so I did."

"But *I'm* not in trouble, and you talk to *me*," Ariadne said, a question in her voice.

May nodded. "I thought you were," she said. "But I was wrong, wasn't I? You weren't really going to run away that day."

"No, I—" Ariadne stopped. "How did you know I was planning to run away?" she asked.

"You wouldn't have done it," May said, as though reassuring her. "It's too dangerous. I told that boy the same thing, and he was still going to do it, but I said that he had to try to get along with his father—"

"What?" Ariadne said through the tightness in her throat. She half rose, her heart pounding. How could May know that she had been thinking of buying a bus ticket and going back to Florida? Ariadne hadn't said a word to anyone.

"I told that boy not to run away," May repeated, as though she hadn't heard Ariadne, "and he went back home, and everything was better."

What boy? But Ariadne wasn't really interested in him. She was much more anxious to discover how May had known that she was thinking of going back to Florida on her own.

"I'm not going to run away," Ariadne said. "But how did you know I was thinking about it that day?"

May rubbed her forehead with her right hand. The locket on her chest glinted coldly when a breeze moved the branch above her and a shaft of sunlight hit it.

"I don't know," she finally said. "There's lots of things I don't know. And lots of things I do. It's—it's like—" She hesitated, looking at Ariadne doubtfully.

"What's it like?" Ariadne asked.

"It's kind of like I know things, but I don't know how. And I'm here, but I'm not here," she said. "I feel like I belong here, and I know things about people here, but I'm someplace else too. I'm between two places. I know this is my home, but I'm still homesick."

"Me too," Ariadne said cautiously. At last May had finally said something that Ariadne could relate to.

"Why are you homesick?" May asked. "Isn't this your home?"

"No," Ariadne said. "Or I suppose in a way it is, since this is where I live. But Florida is really my home, not Tennessee."

"What makes Florida home?" asked May.

"It's just full of everything I know," Ariadne said. Now that May was being normal, she was surprisingly easy to talk to. And she was the only person Ariadne had met here who seemed interested in what she felt. Including her own family.

"I'm not one of those people that moves around a lot and is used to making new friends. Everybody knows me at home and knows what I'm like, so I don't have to stand up in front of a lot of dweebs in a strange classroom and say, 'My name is Ariadne and I just moved here from Florida and I have a brother named Hector.' That's embarrassing and humiliating, and I never want to have to do it again."

She took a big swallow of soda to fight down the tears she felt rising. Jeez, it seemed that every day she either cried or felt like it. It was so stupid. But May didn't seem to mind, or even notice. She put her hand on Ariadne's wrist, and the feel of that light, almost bony touch made all the little hairs on Ariadne's arm stand up. But May didn't seem to notice her reaction.

"I know what that's like," she said softly, as though to herself. "Not the standing up and introducing yourself part, but the not belonging part."

"But you said you've lived here all your life," Ariadne said.

"I have," May said. "But I'm not home."

"How can you not be home if you've lived here all your life?"

May removed her hand, and Ariadne rubbed the place where the thin hand had rested. It had to be her imagination, but her wrist felt cold. Cold and numb. She rubbed harder.

"I can't explain," May said. "But I know I'm not home. And I want to be home." She stopped, whispered, "Sorry," and seemed about to flee into the woods again, but Ariadne grabbed the skirt of her blue dress. It felt flimsy, but at least it wasn't cold.

"Don't go," she said.

May stood still, head bowed, and made no attempt to escape. Ariadne let go of her dress.

"Don't go," she repeated. "Why do you always leave like that?"

"Sometimes I just have to," May said.

"What, is someone calling you?"

"Sort of like that," May said. "I just have to go sometimes."

Weird, thought Ariadne. But not as weird as that hand. I hope she *never* touches me again. "I don't get what you mean—you're home but you want to go home?" she asked.

May said, "That's just how I feel. I don't understand it either. And I don't know how to fix it. And I'm supposed to fix it. I'm the oldest," she said. "I have to take care of everyone. That's what Momma told me before she—" May bit her lip and looked away.

"Before what?" Ariadne said, but May just bowed her head. "Before she went away?" May shook her head.

"Before she died?" Ariadne asked as gently as she could. May nodded.

"But I'm so tired," May said. "And I got lost. I went someplace—" She shook her head again, as though to clear it. "It was dark and I fell . . ." Her voice trailed off, and she rubbed her forehead again.

"What do you mean, you got lost? If you're lost, we have to call the police. Come in the house and let's call. I bet they're looking all over for you. Come on." Ariadne got to her feet.

But May didn't move. Ariadne grew impatient. "Well, either you're lost and we have to find your parents—your father," she amended, "or you're from right here like you told me before and you're not lost. Which is it?"

May spread her hands and looked at Ariadne, and the bleak despair in her face made Ariadne stop talking abruptly.

"I don't know," she whispered. "I just know I'm not home."

"Then where are you?" asked Ariadne, feeling foolish. How could May not know where she was? She was standing right there, wasn't she? Could she be confused—or, well, crazy? Maybe that was it.

"You have to find me," May said. "Ann and Leslie tried but they couldn't find me. You have to look for me and help me go home. I don't know where I am, because I got lost going there. But it's someplace where it's cold in summer and warm in winter. Look for me where it's cold in summer and warm in winter."

"What?" said Ariadne, startled.

At that moment she heard a car pull up, and involuntarily she turned her head toward it. When she looked back at where May had been standing, she saw with no surprise that the spot was empty. The famous disappearing act, Ariadne thought, as she brushed chip crumbs off her green T-shirt. Her hands were trembling, and she stuck them in her shorts pockets so that whoever was in the car couldn't tell. The spot on her wrist was gradually warming up and getting its feeling back.

There's nothing to be afraid of, she told herself firmly as she walked to the driveway. She's just some country girl who's too shy to see more than one person at a time. Or maybe she has some kind of mental problem. But she's not *violent*, Ariadne consoled herself. After all, she took that stinger out, like she cared that I was hurt. She's just confused and a little weird.

But why did a cold shiver run down Ariadne's spine as she turned her back to the shadowy woods? Why did it feel like someone was watching her?

eight

Hector burst out of the car, talking angrily, and didn't even say hello to her.

"Hi, Heck!" she said loudly to show him how rude he'd been. No answer. He just kept arguing with their father, who was letting himself out of the driver's side.

"But all the other kids go hunting!" he said. "It's not fair. Why can't I?"

"You just can't," her father said, and she could tell by his tone that he had already said this a few times on the way home. "You can't go hunting and you can't have a gun, and I won't let you go to anyone's house if there is one."

"What?" Hector said, his voice rising to an indignant squeak. "That means I can't go to practically anyone's house. They *all* have guns."

"Not all of them," her father said. "You can't go to someone's house unless we know there aren't any guns there."

"But—" Hector said.

"Enough. Quit. Be quiet," their father said, and he stomped into the house.

"This sucks," Hector said.

"You'd better not let Dad hear you say that," Ariadne warned him.

"Oh, shut up," he said, and he too stomped off, a miniature version of their father.

Terrific, she thought. How was your day, Ariadne? How was it at a new middle school where you don't know anybody? Lovely how everyone cares.

She sat down on the front steps and finished the chips and salsa. Now what? she thought, and for the first time in her life she wished she had homework. But at that moment Caroline and Ashley pulled up in front of her on their bikes.

"Want to go swimming?" Caroline asked.

"Sure!" Ariadne said. "Let me get on my bathing suit."

"We'll wait for you here, and then walk down the path by your house," said Ashley. "It's the shortest way."

When Ariadne came back out, the others were at the top of the path. She clambered down the steep slope after them, grabbing at thin branches to keep her balance. When they reached the lake, they spread their towels on the big rock at the edge of the water and eased themselves in.

"This way you don't have to walk on the mud," Caroline said.

"Yuck," Ariadne said.

"It's so gross," Ashley said. "And sometimes you find things from the town that used to be down there."

"Yuck," Ariadne said again. "What kind of things?"

"Pieces of metal," Caroline said. "Like old farm tools. And once my dad found some wood that he said used to be a church pew."

"They drowned the church?" Ariadne asked. That didn't seem respectful.

"They drowned *everything*," Caroline said. "Sometimes you can hear the old church bell ringing."

"Yeah, *right*," Ariadne said. But to her surprise, Caroline nodded vigorously.

"You can too," she insisted. "Can't you, Ashley?"

"I heard it once," Ashley agreed. "My mom said it was just a trick of the wind, but I could tell it was the church bell."

"Wow," Ariadne said, and she eased herself into the soupy water. She didn't know whether to believe them. This was just the kind of thing that people told new kids, and then laughed at them when they fell for it. Ashley and Caroline didn't seem like the type to do that, but still, she'd better be careful not to say whether or not she believed them, until she was sure.

They swam around for a few minutes, then hoisted themselves out onto the rock. Ashley painted her white skin all over with sunblock. "Otherwise I'll turn into a boiled crawdad," she explained.

"So what did y'all think of Ms. Saylor?" Caroline asked. Ariadne hesitated; she didn't want to give the first opinion.

Ashley said, "She looks okay. But lots of times they start out that way and turn bad."

"What are you going to do for your social-studies project?" Ariadne asked.

Caroline puffed her cheeks out and sighed. "Who knows? That's the worst part of a project—not doing it, but coming up with the idea for it."

"I think I can find some Web sites that could give us ideas," Ariadne offered.

"Really?" Caroline said. "That would be cool. Want to go look now?"

"No," Ariadne said. "It might take a while. If I find anything good, I'll tell you at school. Or I could e-mail you."

"Cool!" Ashley said. "I wish I could surf the net that easily!"

"It's not so hard," Ariadne said. "It just takes practice, and when we first moved here I didn't have much else to do, so . . ." She didn't finish her sentence.

"Well, now that school's started you won't have that problem," Caroline said. "You'll be too busy with homework," and Ashley groaned in agreement. They lay back, Caroline and Ariadne in the sun, Ashley in the shade. They were silent for a few minutes.

"Are you guys any good at riddles?" Ariadne asked.

"You mean like why did the chicken cross the road?" Caroline said.

"No, I mean the old kind where you have to guess what something is, like what has an eye but can't see, and it turns out to be a needle."

"I don't know," Ashley said. "Never tried it. Give me one."

Ariadne hesitated. Better not ask them the cold-in-summer one right away. So she said, "What goes up a chimney down but not down a chimney up?"

"No idea," Caroline said. "What?"

"An umbrella. When the umbrella's down, it can go up a chimney, but when the umbrella's up, like open, it can't go down a chimney. See?"

"Oh yeah, that's neat," Ashley said. "Up a chimney down, but not down a chimney up. Cool."

"Here's another one," Ariadne said, and she added as casually as she could, "Where is it cold in summer and warm in winter?"

"Fender's Ice Cream," Caroline said promptly.

"*What?*" said the other two.

"Fender's," repeated Caroline. "You know how Mrs.

Harrison keeps it so hot in the winter and so cold in the summer?"

"I think it's an older riddle than that," Ariadne said uncertainly. "I think the answer isn't some specific place like Fender's."

"You *think*?" Caroline said. "You mean you don't know the answer?"

Ariadne hesitated. "I heard someone ask it, but I never heard the answer."

"So how do you know it's an old riddle?"

Good question. "Well, it was—it was an old lady who asked it," said Ariadne, knowing that was a lame answer.

"Warm in summer, and cold in winter—" Caroline said.

"No, you dope," Ashley said. "The other way around. *Cold* in summer, *warm* in winter."

"Oh yeah," Caroline said, and giggled. "Let's see. Think, think, Caroline Kennedy." And she pressed her hands to her temples.

Ashley and Ariadne copied her, and the three sat there intoning, "Think, think," until they all had a fit of the giggles, which only got worse when Ashley said, "My grandmother's house."

"What?" the other two asked together when they'd recovered.

"You know, old people think air-conditioning is such a

wonderful newfangled kind of thang"—she spoke with an exaggerated country twang—"that they keep their house freezing in the summer and hot in the winter."

"It doesn't sound right," Caroline said.

"No, it doesn't," Ariadne said. But what could the answer be? And why wouldn't May just say straight out what she meant? What—or who—was stopping her?

nine

May had been born in Dobbin, but she wasn't home. She was here, but not really here. She needed to be found, but she wasn't lost. And she was someplace where it was cold in summer and warm in winter. Like Fender's Ice Cream—or Ashley's grandmother's house—except Ariadne knew that she really was in the forest.

The girl must be nuts, Ariadne decided as she moved the mouse around on the pad, tracking down Web sites that looked like they might give her an idea for her social-studies project. One looked especially interesting. Maybe she had better grab an idea from it before she passed on the address to the others. It was a government page that showed before-and-after pictures and maps of places around the United States where humans had changed something in the landscape, like carving tunnels through mountains, pumping water out of marshes to make farm-land, making new land with landfill, flooding valleys by building dams. . . .

Flooding valleys by building dams. That might be

something the teacher would like. The whole Cedar Point Lake was formed by a dam, after all, and if there was a way to find out exactly what was covered up by the lake when they did that, she could say something about how governments changed people's lives and made them better for some people and worse for others. Teachers always liked when you did something local, especially when you presented two sides of an argument. And maybe she could track down some people who used to live in the valley and find out how they felt about seeing other people fishing and swimming a hundred feet above the roofs of their old houses.

She clicked on Tennessee, and the drop-down menu listed the dam projects by lake. Center Hill, Old Hickory, Percy Priest—there it was, Cedar Point Lake. Cool! Side by side were two maps, one of the valley before the dam flooded it, and one of the lake after. She clicked to enlarge the picture, and leaned closer to the screen. There weren't a lot of buildings on the before drawing, just twenty or so farms and a church and what was labeled GEN'L STORE. She found the cemetery and hoped that Caroline was right about the bodies being moved. On the after picture was the dam, and the new lake covering the entire valley floor, and a lot more buildings, this time arranged around the edge of the lake. She followed the road around with her finger and stopped where she thought their house must be. Their *rented* house, she reminded herself. As in temporary.

It was the perfect project. It was local, it involved both history and living people, it had some kind of social importance, and it didn't look too hard.

She clicked on some more sites and found old pictures from before the dam. Black and white, of course. There was a family gathered outside a farmhouse, the mother and father on the porch, and the children arranged in size order, like stair steps, in front of them. The oldest, a tall girl in a long skirt, was holding what must be her youngest baby brother or sister. They were squinting into the sun, and no one looked happy. I wonder where that house went to, Ariadne thought. And some of those people must still be alive. Like that baby. Did they take everything out of their house before the lake flooded it?

She opened another one. Here was a school building. It looked kind of like how she thought the Dobbin middle school would be—before she actually saw it, that is. The teacher stood outside, her hand on the rope of a bell. From her stiff posture, it was obvious that she was just posing and wasn't really ringing it. Two fat-cheeked boys stood to one side wearing long-sleeved shirts, even though the sun was glaring down on them, and heavy dark boots. Three little girls, hair in long braids, long dresses reaching down to their feet, stood on the other.

The caption read WPA PROJECT. She clicked on it, and a paragraph came up. "One-room schoolhouse in Taylor

County," she read. "Few children continue past the primary grades, since they are needed to work the poor farms. A new school would—"

"Ariadne!" called her mother. "Log off and leave the phone line free! I'm expecting a call from work."

"Okay!" she called back. Why was her mom's work always more important than hers?

She bookmarked the page, then minimized the Web browser and checked her e-mail again. Nothing. She couldn't believe Sarah hadn't answered her when she knew how traumatized Ariadne had been about starting this country school. All right, so maybe it wasn't as hick as she had thought it would be. But still, Sarah owed her a message, and she'd better write tomorrow. Ariadne logged off.

She went out to the porch, where her parents had taken their wine glasses after dinner. Hector was standing on the flagstones throwing a ball as high as he could. He caught about one in every three tosses. For the other two, he had to race Zephyr to grab the ball before it rolled down the steep slope to the lake.

Ariadne sat down sideways on the glider with her feet on the cushion and wrapped her arms around her knees. "Phone's free," she said.

"Thanks," her mom said, and she took a sip of her wine.

"So what was school like?" her father asked.

"It was like school," Ariadne said.

"Come on," her mother said. "We've heard all about Dobbin Elementary and can recite the names of all the boys in Hector's class, and who plays what sport, plus what his teacher looks like and how strict she is and how the P.E. teacher was almost in the Olympics. Give us a bit of information, Ariadne, just so we know for sure you went there today."

"My homeroom teacher's name is Ms. Saylor, and she's new," Ariadne said.

"Good," her father said. "Now we know one thing. What about the kids?"

Ariadne rested her chin on her knees. "They're okay, I guess," she said. "There aren't many of them, so if you don't like half of them that doesn't leave a whole lot to be friends with."

"Did you see those girls you went to get ice cream with?"

"Yes, Mom, of *course* I did. There are only twenty kids in the whole seventh grade, so how could I not see them?"

"Sweetie, calm down. I just don't know anyone else to ask about. I haven't met any of your other friends."

"That's because I don't *have* any other friends. I wish you had let me move in with Sarah. Her parents would have said it was okay if you did." But Ariadne's familiar protest was half hearted. She knew when she had lost.

"Yeah, you should have let her stay with Sarah,"

Hector said. Ariadne hadn't even noticed that he was listening. "She's gotten so lonely she goes out in the woods and talks to herself."

"I do not!" Ariadne said.

"You do too," Hector said. "You go out in the woods and talk just like someone was there, but there isn't anyone. You've gone crazy."

"Hush, Hector," their father said. "Don't tease. Ariadne can talk to herself if she wants."

"But I don't!" Ariadne said. "I only talk when there's someone there. Like today I went swimming with Caroline and Ashley. I talked to them, but they were there the whole time and they answered me. You're the one who's crazy, Hector. And I wish you'd quit spying on me."

"I don't mean today," Hector said. "I mean the day we had that picnic at the lake. You went off in the woods and started talking when there was no one there."

"There was too someone there!" Ariadne said. "And anyway, why were you following me?"

"I had to pee," Hector said.

"So pee in the lake like everyone else!" Ariadne said. "You're always following me. Mom, you said you'd make him stop."

"I wasn't following you," Hector said. "And anyway, I don't like to pee in the lake. It's not exactly *private*. Those jet-skis zoom up to you. But all I was doing was looking for a private place to pee in the woods and there you were talking to someone. But there wasn't anyone there."

"Hector," their mother said. "Ariadne can talk to herself if she wants, just like Dad said. Leave her alone and quit following her. She needs her space."

"But Mom!" Ariadne said. "I was *not* talking to myself. There was a girl there. Hector probably just didn't see her because she's very quiet and kind of hides in the bushes."

"Oh, sure—" Hector began, but their father turned on him and said, "One more word about this, young man, and you go to your room," so Hector shut up. He stuck out his tongue at Ariadne when their parents weren't looking, but she pretended not to see him. What a moron, she thought. She hadn't been that childish when she was ten.

"What were you working at so hard on the Internet, Addy?" her father asked in an obvious attempt to change the subject.

"Finding a topic for my social-studies project," she answered.

"Wow!" her mother said. "The first day of school and they already assigned a project! I had heard Polk was a tough school, but that seems to be taking it a bit far."

"They didn't actually assign it yet," Ariadne said. "I just want to get a head start so the others don't grab all the good ideas."

"So what did you come up with?" her father asked. Ariadne told them about the dam and the lake.

"Excellent," her mother said. "Let me talk to some people in the history department at the college and see if I can get you some information."

"No," Ariadne said. "Don't do that, Mom. I want this to be all my own project. I can find what I need on the Internet and in that little library."

"Good," her father said. "Do it all yourself. Just be sure to check it out with your teacher before you get started. She may want you to do Ancient Egypt or something."

"Ancient Egypt was last year," she said. "At least in Florida it was. In seventh grade you do your own state. And I guess for now that's Tennessee."

"It sure is," her mother said. "Up to bed, now, both of you. School again tomorrow, and this time it's going to be a full day."

Ariadne said good night and went up the stairs to her room with the slanted ceiling. She lay in bed and looked at the stars through the skylight. What did Hector mean, she was talking to herself? May was small and blended in with the woods, but hadn't he seen her?

Or maybe he was right and she was losing her mind, talking to nonexistent people, like crabby Mrs. Harrison. Or cranky Jade Kennedy.

Or maybe Hector was just being a jerk.

Or—and she tried not to think it, but the thought wouldn't go away—maybe there was something about May that made her invisible to everyone but Ariadne. No, she told herself. That's impossible. Plus she said she had two other friends.

Two other friends that no one seemed to have heard of.

ten

Ms. Saylor liked Ariadne's social-studies idea and seemed impressed that she was getting started on her project so early. "I know it's tough being new," she said, "and finding out about this area might make you feel more at home here." Ariadne nodded. She hadn't thought of it that way, but maybe the teacher was right. Ms. Saylor was new too, after all.

Ms. Saylor told her to read up on the reunion of the people who used to live in the valley. That way she might be able to get some firsthand interviews. The county had a weekly newspaper, but it wasn't online, so she had to go to the library to get the back issues.

She went after school on Friday. The library was tiny, just an old house on the town square. The librarian showed Ariadne where the back issues of the newspapers were. "What exactly are you looking for?" he asked.

"The reunion they have for the people who lived in the valley before the dam was built," she said. "I'm doing something on it for my social-studies project."

"Good topic," he said. "You shouldn't have trouble locating it. Not much happens around here, so the reunion is always front-page news."

It didn't take Ariadne long to find what she was looking for. The librarian glanced down at the sheaf of papers in her hand as she stood at the copier.

"Found it already, I see," he said. She nodded, then copied a page and ran a yellow highlighter over the names of the people who had shown up at last year's reunion.

"Can I take a look?" the librarian asked. Ariadne pushed the paper across the table. "You could find lots of these folks in town, I think. Some of them were just kids when the dam was built, and so they're in their sixties and seventies now. You should be able to find them with no trouble." He ran his finger down the list. "Miss Lois Cartwright, Mrs. Ann F. Harrison, Mrs. Alice Spivey—" he broke off. "All women. I guess it's true what they say, that you females live longer than us poor males. No, here's one man, anyway: Mr. Mackenzie L. Frank."

"How can I find if any of them are still here?"

"Phone book," he said.

Duh, Ariadne thought. "Do you have one here?"

He pulled one out from under the desk. "Let's see if I can help," he said. "I know most everybody around here." He ran his finger down her list as he flipped through the pages.

"Miss Cartwright died last winter, so you can scratch her off. I don't know Mrs. Spivey. I bet she lives out of the area, but you might try to find her at the reunion this year. Mrs. Harrison owns Fender's Ice Cream. She must have been pretty young when they made the dam."

"Oh, I've met her," Ariadne said. "But—" She stopped and blushed.

"But you don't want to interview her?" he asked, and when she nodded, he said, "I know—she's not terribly friendly. But maybe if she starts talking about the old days she'll be nicer. You never know." He continued looking at the list. "Mr. Frank lives with his daughter in the trailer park out on Highway 32. His hearing is gone and his mind isn't all there, but often elderly people remember the olden times better than what happened this morning. You might want to give him a try, but call first and make sure his daughter says it's okay." He pointed to the correct Frank in the phone book, and she wrote down the number.

"Thanks," said Ariadne, gathering up her notes. "I guess there are some advantages to living in a small town where you know everybody."

"Lots," the librarian said. "I wouldn't live anyplace else." That's because you probably never tried anyplace else, thought Ariadne. "Have you thought about what questions to ask?" he went on.

"No," she answered. "I thought I'd just say things like 'What difference did the dam make in your life?' "

"You're not going to get many good answers that way," he said. "They'll probably just talk about how the world is different and won't get too specific about what changes the dam made and what changes would have happened anyway in sixty years. You should really do some research on what life was like here before the dam so you can ask better questions."

"Well, okay, I guess so," she said. "Where should I look?"

"Local history," he said. "I'll show you."

He squatted down in front of a shelf and started pulling old books off it. "I can't remember when anyone checked these out last," he said.

She picked one up. *"A History of Taylor County, Tennessee, from King's Mountain to the Present,"* she read. "What's King's Mountain?"

"That's right, you're not from here," he said. "It's a Revolutionary War battle that a lot of Tennesseans fought in, even though there wasn't a Tennessee yet. We're very proud of it."

She looked in the front of the book. The "present" of the title was 1926, so the dam wouldn't even have been thought of yet. She had already learned that it had been built in 1937. Still, it should give her some idea of what kind of things were happening at the time. She couldn't imagine that anything changed very fast in those days, especially here. She was about to leave when she caught sight of another book, poking out of the shelf a little bit. She pulled it out and opened it. Its pages were less crumbly than the other one. *Taylor Tales: Colorful Residents of Taylor County, Tennessee.* It didn't look like it would have much to do with her project, so she put it back and went to the desk with the first one.

After she folded up her photocopied pages and notes and put them in her backpack, she glanced down the aisle where she had gotten the history book. There, lying on the floor, was that other book, the colorful-tales one. She was sure she had put it back on the shelf. Why was it lying on the floor?

She didn't want the librarian to think she was a slob, so she went back and picked it up. She looked for the empty space on the shelf, to slide it back in the right spot, but there wasn't one. Weird.

A soft voice, so close to her ear that it made the little hairs inside tickle, said with great intensity, *"Take it."*

"What?" she said involuntarily.

The librarian looked up. "You say something?"

Ariadne looked around. There was no one there but the two of them. She swallowed hard.

"Who else came in?" she asked.

The librarian looked puzzled. "No one," he said. "I would have heard the bell ring, even if I didn't see the door open."

Ariadne glanced over her shoulder, thinking that maybe one of the kids from school had come in and was playing some kind of stupid trick on her. But she didn't see anyone. It must have been her imagination. Still, that voice had sounded so *real.*

Cut it out, she told herself firmly. That librarian was talking to himself and was embarrassed to admit it. Or some other noise had sounded like a voice. Just forget it. Only crazy people heard things that weren't there.

She forced herself to look at the book in her hand as though nothing had happened. There was nothing out of the ordinary about it, except that it looked old. She opened to the title page and saw that it was from 1946. Maybe a few people who still lived in Dobbin had known some of those colorful residents. Oh well, might as well check it out. And it's *not* because something told me to, she told herself. It's because it will be useful for my report. I think.

"Thanks a lot," she said as the librarian took the old book and the other ones from her. "These should give me a good start. I don't have a library card yet, but—"

"Oh, that's okay," he said. "Just fill out a form and you can take out up to five books."

After dinner she checked her e-mail. Finally, a message from Sarah. But it was disappointing.

Dear Ariadne, I'm glad you're liking your new school and the kids. I hope you don't get tired of them too fast. My mom says to say hello to your mom. Sarah

What did she mean by getting tired of the kids here? She wasn't in the mood to answer, and what could she say to that message, anyway? And why was it so weird, without even their little heart symbol? So she logged off and opened the library books.

The one that the librarian had recommended had a lot about Dobbin's history but not much about how the people in the valley had lived. Still, she took some notes on the population, farming, and things like that.

She opened the next book. There were chapters about famous people who came from Taylor County, such as Civil War generals (on both sides) and some guy who wrote a bird book. Most of the ordinary people in it were the kind who nowadays would get locked up in a loony bin, but the author seemed to find them charming. In fact, that was his favorite word. The man who tamed squirrels and had twenty in his house, the preacher who thought that everyone should come to church naked (including himself, but he probably had a pulpit or whatever in front of him), the woman who had fourteen sons and named the last one Lucille because that was her favorite name and she had given up on ever having a daughter—they were all *charming*. Yuck. So she closed it and picked up the last one.

She turned the pages, trying to find something useful. But this book wasn't arranged in chronological order, and there was no index, so she had to go through page by page. One chapter was entitled "Mysteries and Mischief."

Probably Halloween tales, and sure enough, there were the ghosts, the mysterious voices, the black cats—all the stuff you would expect. She flipped the pages faster, hoping to find something she could use.

Nothing.

She closed the book and held it in both hands, staring down at it. What had made her turn back and look at it? And who had told her to take it?

No one, she told herself firmly. That librarian was probably talking to himself. That didn't explain why she felt the voice right in her ear while the librarian was across the room, though. Some trick, she thought, or strange acoustics or whatever it was called. It couldn't be anything else. Anyway, she wasn't like Mrs. Harrison. She didn't talk to people who weren't there. *She* wasn't crazy.

Ariadne had relaxed her grip on the book, and it fell open naturally, as though some earlier reader had turned to the same spot again and again. She glanced down, and what she saw on the yellowing page made her skin jump. No! she thought, and slammed it shut. That couldn't be what it said! She sat still until the pounding of her heart slowed.

I'll just take it back to the library, she thought. Right now. They must have a book drop. Or I'll leave it against the door, and the librarian can take it in when he opens. If nobody steals bikes here, surely they won't steal a dusty old book.

But even as she reached for her backpack, she realized she couldn't do it. She had to know.

Slowly, reluctantly, she let the book fall open again.

She hadn't imagined it. She sat with her mouth open and stared at the heavy black letters.

"The Strange Case of Little May Butler."

eleven

"Ariadne!" her mother called up the stairs. "Want to play poker?"

She couldn't answer.

"Ariadne!"

She put down the book slowly. What had her mother said? Oh yes, poker.

"No!" she shouted.

"Oh, come on!" her father joined in. "We can't play poker with just three people."

"So play something else!"

"What TV show is so fascinating?"

Honestly, was that all they thought she did? She went to the top of the stairs and called down, "I'm not watching TV."

She heard Hector say, "Oh, sure."

"I'm doing research for my social-studies project, and I just found something really interesting. Can't I please stay up here and work on it some more?"

"That's the first time I've ever heard you ask to spend

more time on your homework," her father said. "Go for it. We'll play cribbage."

She heard Hector grumble, "I *hate* cribbage," and her father say, "Let's play two against one, and maybe we'll beat your mother for once," and then their voices faded as they went into the den. Good. They would stay busy for a while. Just explaining the rules to Hector again should take twenty minutes. She went back to her room and closed the door.

"The Strange Case of Little May Butler," she read again. Her fingers left little sweat marks on the thick pages.

> *The Butlers were once among the most important families in this region, the first, Ansel Butler, having settled with his wife and four sons in the eastern part of Taylor County sometime before 1770. His oldest son, James Butler, distinguished himself in the Battle of King's Mountain (1780) and upon his return from the war made a decent living in the fertile land at the basin of the hollow that is now covered by Cedar Point Lake.*
>
> *None of James Butler's descendants made a success of farming, and the family gradually sank into poverty. Nothing of note occurred until the time of the great-grandchildren of James Butler in the mid-1850s. By now the descendants of Ansel Butler's four*

sons occupied many of the farms in the neighborhood. The poorest farm belonged to Hiram Butler, the oldest of whose three children was a girl named Jane May, called May to distinguish her from her mother, who bore the same name.

The family was nearly destitute, despite the father's best efforts to provide for them, since he had the misfortune to inherit the rockiest and least productive land of all the descendants. His wife had two children before May, but both died in infancy, as did the baby boy born when May was one year old. Accordingly, the parents were more than usually anxious for the surviving children, and May appears to have inherited their eager watchfulness, for she took charge of her brother and sister (Andrew and Cecilia) when her mother fell ill after the birth of the latter, and was said to have expended much care on their behalf. When the mother died a year later, little May seems to have been given sole care of the younger children.

Ariadne stopped reading as a creepy feeling settled into her stomach. What had that girl said? Something about her mother telling her she had to look out for the others. And this Jane May from the nineteenth century also seemed to be the responsible type. Looking out for people. Helping them. Ariadne shook her head. Too much of a weird coin-cidence. It was spooky. And anyway, it didn't have any-thing to do with her social-studies paper.

Forget it, she thought, and closed the book. Maybe May was a descendant of that girl in the book. People do get named for their ancestors, after all. So maybe she was trying to act like her great-great-grandmother, or whatever she was.

Or maybe—maybe someone was playing a practical joke on her. That would explain that voice in the library. They were trying to scare her because she was new—that was it!

Anger replaced her uneasiness. Well, if that's what they were trying to do, they wouldn't succeed. She wasn't afraid of any stupid story about some person who lived hundreds of years ago. To prove it, she picked up the book again. She would just finish reading the chapter, find out what hap-pened to this nineteenth-century May Butler, and forget about it.

So when May did not reappear from a berrying expedition one evening in her twelfth year, her father was instantly concerned that some accident had befallen her. She had never absented herself from her duties before, and he knew that there must be some dire reason for her absence. Further, he was concerned that the gold locket she wore, her only legacy from her mother, might have tempted some thief to kill her for it.

For hours the anxious father and his neighbors scoured the woods. The river was also searched. The hunt was not successful, however, and Hiram was forced to the sad conclusion that his child had been either kidnapped by a passing stranger, or taken by a bear or other wild animal. And indeed her body was never found.

Imagine his heartbreak, then, when some months after his older daughter's disappearance, his youngest child, Cecilia, also vanished. The scene was repeated, with the frantic father and all the neighbors combing the woods for the little girl, aided only by the weak light of lanterns. Once again, however, the hunt was not successful, and Butler returned to his cabin heart-sick. As he stepped through the doorway, his boot touched a heap on the threshold, and to his astonishment he saw that it was the sleeping form of his little Cecilia. He caught her up in his arms and rushed her into the house, where he examined his precious child and found her to be in perfect condition.

When questioned as to where she had been, the little girl, her speech still being imperfect, was unable to make any response that her anxious parent could *understand. But when she was asked how she had found her way home, her answer was clear enough to strike a chill in the heart of her interrogator.*

"May find me," she said, and no matter how many times she was questioned, and how many times her father reminded her of the punishment for lying, she repeated, "May find me. May bring me home."

And that was not the last of it. Several years later a boy who was running away from a harsh father came home reporting that a "girl in the woods" had convinced him to try to make peace with his family, and indeed, when he returned, the boy found his father so shaken at his disappearance that the beatings ceased.

Similar sightings were reported for the rest of the century, occasionally by a boy, but mostly by girls at the threshold of womanhood. No adult ever reported seeing May, and many of those who, as children, claimed that they had seen her, later said that they had merely been playing childish games, and that no such apparition had ever made itself visible.

Ariadne stared at the page until tears of anger made the words blur. Childish games. That's what she would call it, all right. And she had thought the others were so nice. What did they do, find some pathetic girl, dress her up in old-fashioned clothes, and stake her out in the woods to try to convince Ariadne that she was nuts? They must have known that sooner or later she'd talk to someone about meeting someone odd in the forest, and then they'd all have a good laugh at the new girl's expense.

She felt herself blush at the memory of asking Caroline if she had ever heard of a girl named May Butler. Her sister, Jade, must have been in on it too to have acted the way she did.

Well, they would have to get their laughs somewhere else. The next time Ariadne saw that "May" girl, she'd tell her she knew what was up, and that she should go find some other new kid who would fall for her act. She had seen through their trick, and it was a crummy thing to do. She slammed the book shut and tried to blink the tears out of her eyes. But they spilled over and ran down her cheeks, tickling until she rubbed at them angrily.

Sarah was the only one she could tell, the only one who wouldn't laugh. She opened her dresser drawer and counted the money she had saved up. Almost fifty dollars, including the twenty from Grandma for her birthday. She blew her nose and wiped the tear tracks off her face.

She went down to the den, where the rest of the family was playing cards. They had given up on cribbage and were playing I Doubt It.

"Mom?" she said, hanging back in the doorway, where she hoped no one could see her face clearly.

"Three kings!" her mother said, and instantly, of course, her father started singing, "We three kings of Orient are."

"What, honey? You want to play? You can take over my hand."

"No, Mom," she said. She suddenly felt hollow inside. "I want to call Sarah."

"Three aces," Hector said.

"Addy, we talked about long-distance calls," her father said. "Why not e-mail her?"

Ariadne ignored him. "I have almost fifty dollars saved up," she said, and her voice caught a little. She talked louder to keep from crying again. She didn't want her parents feeling bad for her and trying to cheer her up. That would just make it worse. "I could pay you back."

Ariadne's mother put down her cards and looked at her. "You okay, sweetie?" she asked.

Ariadne nodded. "Fine," she said. "I just want to talk to Sarah."

Now her father was looking at her too. "Go ahead," he said. "Don't worry about paying us back." And he turned to the game. "Let's see," he said. "You had kings, Betsy, and then you did aces, Heck, so it's deuces to me. One deuce." And he slid a card onto the stack.

Hector leaped up and did a victory dance. "I put down *all* my cards and said three aces! And no one doubted it because you were talking to Ariadne! I'm out, I'm out, I'm out!" He danced around the table and planted a big wet kiss on Ariadne's cheek. "Thank you, thank you, thank you!"

She grimaced and wiped her face. "You're welcome," she said, and went to her dad's study, closing the door behind her.

Her fingers dialed Sarah's number automatically. Sarah's mother answered.

"Hi, it's Ariadne," she said.

"Ariadne! Hey, how are you?"

"I'm okay," she said. "Is Sarah home?"

"She's right here. She heard me say your name, and I'm having to fight to keep the phone away from her. Here she is—give your mom and dad a big kiss for me."

"Okay," she said, and then there was Sarah.

"Ariadne!" she said.

"Oh, God, Sarah," she said, "I can't believe how good it is to hear your voice. This place *sucks*."

"But I thought you loved it there," said Sarah.

"Why on earth would you think that?"

"You keep writing about that great virtual learning center or whatever, and how nice that Caroline person is, and Ashley—"

"Well, I was wrong," Ariadne said.

"I thought that meant you were tired of me. And you never once said you missed me."

"And *you* never said you missed *me.*"

"Well, I do," Sarah said.

"And I do too. I can't wait until Thanksgiving. You're still coming, aren't you?"

"Absolutely," Sarah said, "now that I know you still want me."

Twelve

They talked for almost an hour. Suddenly the whole May Butler trick didn't seem very important, so Ariadne didn't tell Sarah about it, but she did say that the kids liked to make fun of new people. Sarah told her how Jeffy Bigelow had dyed his hair blue and his father had grounded him for a month. Mr. McGerr was nice, but he really piled the work on.

Ariadne finally hung up the phone and stared at it for a moment. It was amazing how much better she felt. When she breathed, it seemed like she was really filling her lungs for the first time since they had moved to Tennessee. She stretched and relished the feeling. Had she been too tense even to stretch in these last few weeks?

She went back into the den. "Where's Hector?" she asked.

"Went to bed half an hour ago. And you need to go up too," her mother said. But Ariadne settled down on the sofa next to her.

"How's Sarah?" her mother asked, putting her arm lightly around Ariadne's shoulder.

"Fine," Ariadne said. Her mom's arm felt good, despite the fact that lately Ariadne hadn't really liked anyone touching her. "Her mom said to give you guys a big kiss."

"Make it a good-night kiss," her father said. So she kissed them both good night and went up to her room.

The next day was Saturday. As good a day as any to start interviewing people for her project, especially since she sure wasn't going to hang out with Caroline or Ashley. They had let her know what they thought of her by playing that trick, and she was going to let them know what she thought of them by having nothing to do with them.

The woman who answered the phone at Mr. Frank's house said she was his daughter. Once she understood that nobody was trying to sell her anything, she invited Ariadne to come out and talk to her father. "Although once you get him started, it will be hard to stop him," she warned, "especially if you get him talking about the war."

Ariadne rode her bike up through town, then down the other side of the ridge to Highway 32. The trailer park was easy to spot, and Mr. Frank's daughter had told her to look for the "home with the green awning." She parked her bike and knocked on the metal door.

A large, middle-aged woman opened the door for her and said, "Come on in, honey; don't let the cool air out." Ariadne stepped in and blinked to adjust her eyes to the darkness. The woman said, "So you're the little girl who's doing the paper on Dobbin before the dam?" Ariadne nodded. "I'm Mrs. Unser, Mr. Frank's daughter. Ever since I told Pop about it, he's been excited. He always wants to talk about those days, but I'm afraid I don't really listen. You'll have to speak up, honey. His ears aren't much good anymore, and he doesn't want to wear those hearing aids I got him."

Ariadne blinked again and saw an old man huddled in an armchair watching TV. He was wearing an orange baseball cap that said VOLS in big white letters across the front. Mrs. Unser said, "Now, don't be shy, honey. Come on— I'll tell him you're here." She leaned over to the old man and said loudly, "Pop. Pop," and the man turned and smiled up at her. "Here's the little girl I told you about. Now don't talk her ear off; you want her to get a good grade on her paper."

"That's right," the old man said, and he turned a beaming smile on Ariadne. "Get an A on your paper and dedicate it to Mack Frank!"

He seems like a nice old guy, she thought, and relaxed a little.

"Thanks for seeing me, Mr. Frank," she began.

"Speak up, honey," the woman encouraged her.

"Thanks for seeing me, Mr. Frank," she said louder, and he nodded eagerly. She explained what she was writing about, but before she had a chance to ask any questions, he launched into a description of daily life in the valley before 1937.

"I was born in nineteen and twenty-one. Write that down," he instructed. "Nineteen and twenty-one. My poppa was a soldier in World War I and fought alongside of Alvin York." Ariadne wrote that down too since he seemed so proud of it and made a mental note to find out who Alvin York was. "We were farmers, like everybody else. We started working in the field as soon as we could walk."

"What did you grow?" she asked.

"Well, everybody had a vegetable garden where they grew for the family. And most everybody kept pigs. The only cash crop most of us had was tobacco. Some people tried cotton, but you need a lot of flat land for that, same as for corn. Not enough room in the hollow for either one of those. So we grew enough tobacco to sell for things we couldn't grow ourselves, like shoes." He chuckled. "Never did see a shoe vine, did you?"

"No, sir," Ariadne said, but he hadn't waited for her answer.

"And coffee," he said. "And sugar. We used honey for sweetening most of the time, but my momma dearly loved real sugar in her coffee." Ariadne took notes and looked around the trailer. Some framed color photographs of heavyset people squinting in the sun, a collection of china ducks, some embroidered pillows. Nothing that looked like it was from before the dam.

She realized that Mr. Frank had stopped talking. "Sounds like hard work," she said, hoping he had still been talking about farming, and to her relief he nodded and leaned toward her, emphasizing his words with his finger jabbing the air.

"It was," he said. "It was terrible hard work. You count your blessings, young lady, that you can go to a nice school and go swimming with your friends on the weekends. That's the way it should be. You should play when you're young and work when you're grown."

"Was it all hard work?" Ariadne asked. "Don't you miss anything from those days?"

"Well, yes, of course I do," he said. "I miss going to church with my family on Sundays. The church up here doesn't feel right to me. It's too new, and I don't think it's right to bury all the folks from the old graveyard in one hole."

"Pop, most of those bones had gotten all jumbled together in the old cemetery anyway," Mrs. Unser said. Mr. Frank ignored her.

"And I miss the music," he said. "We didn't have

any television set, of course, and not even a radio until after I came back from the war. Did I tell you I was in the army?"

Mrs. Unser broke in again, shooting a humorous glance at Ariadne. "She's not interested in that, Pop. Tell her about the music."

"Seemed like everybody knew how to play something," he said, and Ariadne and Mrs. Unser exchanged smiles, relieved that she had successfully headed him off. "Poppa played the banjo, and one of the neighbors had a fiddle. We'd get together on cold nights and dance to keep ourselves warm. You ever see clogging, young lady?" Ariadne shook her head and looked at Mrs. Unser.

"It's old-timey country dancing," she explained. "Kind of like tap dancing."

"Nothing like tap dancing," he said. "If I could get up from this chair, I'd show you clogging!" And his feet shuffled on the floor.

"Now, don't get excited, Pop," Mrs. Unser said, and the old man settled back.

"What else?" Ariadne asked.

"We used to tell stories on winter nights when it got dark too early to stay outside. Nobody tells stories anymore."

"We have the TV, Pop," Mrs. Unser said.

He shook his head. "It's not the same. Now all those

stories have been lost. The only people who know them anymore are old, and we're forgetting them since we don't have anyone interested to tell them to." He glared at his daughter, who ignored him. He sighed. "When we die, the tales will be gone forever."

Ariadne decided to change the subject. There was something she really wanted to know. She wanted to find out if that story about May Butler had been true. She didn't know why it was so important to her, but it was. She felt her heart begin to pound as she asked, "Did you know all the neighbors?"

"Know them? Of course I knew them. There weren't many people in the hollow, and we all went to church together on Sunday and to school in the winter."

"Did you know anybody—" Her nerves got the better of her, and she stopped. She cleared her throat and went on. "Did you know anybody named Butler?"

"My grandmother was a Butler before she married Grandfather," said the old man. "But she was the last one. There used to be lots of them in the valley, though."

Well, that hadn't gotten her very far. "So what else did you do for fun, besides dancing and telling stories?"

"We all knew the woods like nobody's business," he said. "We would go hunting berries, and looking for hogs that had escaped, and exploring."

"Were there still Indians here then?"

Mrs. Unser gave a snort of laughter, and the old man turned and shot her a fierce glare, and she stopped.

"Don't laugh at the little girl," he said. "She can ask me anything she wants."

"But it's not like you could meet up with Davy Crockett or Daniel Boone at the general store when you were a boy," she said. "Kids today—"

"Know a lot more than *some* people give them credit for," he said, and then turned pointedly back to Ariadne, who was so embarrassed at being the cause of this family friction that she hardly dared to breathe.

"They weren't living wild in the hills, if that's what you mean," he said. "But there were plenty of people with Indian blood in them in these parts when I was a youngster. Even some Melungeons, though they're mostly in Kentucky. Still are some Indians here, I'd wager. This was where the Cherokee lived before President Jackson ran them off. You heard of the Trail of Tears?"

Ariadne nodded, still trying not to look in Mrs. Unser's direction.

"Some of 'em hid out when the soldiers came to round them up. They hid in the houses of white people who were kin to them, and in caves, and some in the basement of the church where the soldiers didn't think of looking. Then when things cooled off, out they came again."

"Caves?" Ariadne said.

"Lord yes, honey," said Mrs. Unser. "These hills are

like an old Swiss cheese, just full of caves. A sinkhole opened up on the ridge road last year, and when you dropped a rock in it, you could count to five before it hit bottom. It was that deep."

"I've never seen a cave," Ariadne said.

"Get your folks to take you up to Mammoth Cave," Mrs. Unser said. "We went there on a school trip when I was a girl, and I've never forgotten it. I hear they found the bones of some poor Indian who was crushed by a rock thousands of years ago."

Mr. Frank had been looking from one to the other with obviously growing impatience.

"Hey, who's being interviewed here, you or me?" he broke in.

Mrs. Unser gave Ariadne a wry smile.

"You, Pop," she said.

"So let the little girl ask me more questions. Come on, honey, I'm getting tired. And my TV show is coming on in a few minutes. What else do you want to know?"

How could she bring the conversation around to May Butler without just coming right out and asking him? She glanced down at her notes. Food, church, entertainment—

"What kind of stories did people tell before there was radio?" she asked.

"Oh, lord, I've forgotten them all," he said. "There were Jack tales, I recall. But I can't remember how any of them went. And I don't think Susie ever heard them, did you?" he asked his daughter. She shook her head.

"Afraid not, honey," she said to Ariadne. "The radio came in and then everyone from the valley moved away from each other, and then we got TV, and most of the old stories got lost."

Ariadne took a deep breath. It was now or never. She forced herself to say, as casually as she could, "Did you ever hear a story about a little girl, a girl who got lost in the woods?"

Mr. Frank's eyes suddenly narrowed, and he leaned forward, his hands gripping the arms of his chair. "Now, where did you hear about that?" he asked.

"So you know the story?" Ariadne asked.

"What story?" Mrs. Unser said. "Pop, what are you talking about?"

He leaned back again. "Lord, little May Butler. I haven't thought of that story for years and years," he said.

"Pop!" Mrs. Unser said. "What are you talking about?"

"Just an old tale," Mr. Frank said. "A sad tale. I don't want to talk about it."

"That's okay," Ariadne said, and she touched his hand tentatively. "It's just that I wondered if any of those old stories still got told after the dam was built, or if everybody watched TV instead. We don't have to talk about May Butler if you don't want to."

"I can tell you the answer to that," Mrs. Unser broke in. "I never heard a story about anyone named May Butler, and I grew up here."

That was strange. If Mrs. Unser had never heard the story, how had Caroline and Ashley? No one but Ms. Saylor knew what she had chosen for her social-studies project. And if she hadn't heard that voice, or whatever it was, she never would have found that book and would never have read about May Butler. So their little trick wouldn't have worked. Ariadne would just have thought the strange girl was someone who lived in the woods and was home-schooled. Or a Mennonite, like her mother had said.

Mr. Frank was already fumbling with the remote. She stood up. "Thank you for your time, Mr. Frank. You've really helped me."

He punched a button and the TV came to noisy life, with canned laughter. He must be tired, Ariadne thought. Or maybe he just wants to get rid of me.

Mrs. Unser walked Ariadne to the door. "Don't mind Pop," she said. "He gets that way sometimes."

"It's okay," Ariadne said. "It was really nice of him to talk to me. And you too," she added hastily.

"Who else are you planning on talking to about the old town?" Mrs. Unser asked. "Maybe I know some of them."

Ariadne pulled her list out of her pocket. "Ann F. Harrison," she read.

Mr. Frank's hearing suddenly seemed to have improved.

"No Harrisons around here when the dam was built," he grumbled.

"That's Ann Fender," Mrs. Unser told him. "Pop, she got married years ago, and her married name is Harrison."

"And a good thing too," he said. "The way her parents treated that poor girl, I hope she found herself a nice man." He switched channels on the TV.

Mrs. Unser stepped outside with Ariadne and pulled the screen door shut behind her. "I told you he lives in the past," she said. "Ann Harrison was married forty years ago and divorced real soon afterwards. And from what I hear, her husband wasn't any nicer to her than her parents were."

"What did they do?" Ariadne asked.

"Well, it's not a secret. Everyone around here knows what they were like," Mrs. Unser said. "And it's too bad they didn't call it child abuse in those days and have special phone numbers for children to call. They were purely cruel to that girl, honey. Beat her and locked her up and Lord knows what else. And she was all alone; she had no brothers or sisters, and she was so scared and shy that she didn't have any friends. She was a young woman when I was a child, but even then I could see the sadness in her eyes. It's no wonder she's grown so sour."

Ariadne got on her bike. "Thanks again," she said, and raised her hand in farewell. She aimed a wave at the window too, although she figured that Mr. Frank was probably watching his TV and wouldn't see her. But as she glanced back over her shoulder to check for cars before getting on the drive, she saw his face peering out the window at her, the cap pushed back slightly on his head. It was too dark to be sure, but from his expression, it looked as though he were sending her a warning. Why? she wondered, and for a moment was tempted to go back inside and ask him. But then the face disappeared.

The day had grown hot, so Ariadne pumped her legs slowly. How strange. How very, very strange. Now that she thought about it, she had to admit that Caroline and the others couldn't have had anything to do with the girl who called herself May Butler. She had just been made paranoid by that terribly uncomfortable first day as a new girl. She was suddenly fervently grateful that she hadn't accused them of trying to trick her.

That old guy was neat. And he wasn't much older than her own grandfather, who had grown up in a city and had had a radio and a car and had gone to college. Mr. Frank might as well have been born in 1821, not 1921. Maybe that dam was a good thing if bringing electricity here meant that children could go to school instead of work in tobacco fields.

Soon she found herself in the town square. She walked her bike to the cemetery and looked down at the pinkish stone that showed the names of the people from the old graveyard. There was Ansel Butler and James Butler and lots of other Butlers. But no Hiram, Jane May, Andrew, or Cecilia. No Butler had been buried there for more than one hundred years. Well, after all, Mr. Frank had said that his grandmother was the last one.

She could dimly see Mrs. Harrison through the window of her store. Ariadne got back on her bike to ride away, then stopped and leaned on one foot. Should she ask about May now, before she lost her nerve? She took a deep breath and got off her bike, then leaned it up against a wall.

Luckily no one else was in Fender's just then, although she could see some people licking cones as they walked down the sidewalk. Better go in now before another customer came by.

She pushed the door open. Caroline was right; it was awfully cold in there after the heat outside. She felt goose bumps rising on her arms.

"Decided what you want?" asked Mrs. Harrison, without even giving her a chance to look around. But Ariadne didn't really care what she had. Her heart was thumping.

"Mint chocolate chip in a sugar cone, please," she said. As Mrs. Harrison scooped it out, Ariadne took a deep breath and blurted, "I'm doing a social-studies project at Polk Middle School about how life has changed since the dam was built, and I wanted to know if I could ask you some questions." With any luck, Mrs. Harrison's well-known crankiness would take over, and she would say no, and then Ariadne wouldn't have to bother with Mrs. Grouch at all. Or with finding out about May Butler.

But Mrs. Harrison picked up a rag and wiped the counter. "What do you want to know?" she asked.

Ariadne had been so sure that Mrs. Harrison would say no that she hadn't thought of what to ask. So she said the first thing that came into her mind.

"Did you ever hear the story of May Butler?" she asked.

Mrs. Harrison dropped her cloth and leaned heavily on the counter with both hands. Then she looked deep into Ariadne's eyes with her ice blue ones.

"You've seen her, haven't you?" she whispered. Ariadne's mouth went dry, and she felt paralyzed. The goose bumps on her arms were not from cold anymore.

Thirteen

Ariadne stared at Mrs. Harrison. She saw that the woman's eyes were filling with tears. Abruptly, Mrs. Harrison picked up her cloth and slapped it on the counter.

"We're closed," she announced.

"C-c-closed?" Ariadne stammered.

Mrs. Harrison didn't answer but went to the door and firmly turned the sign around. "Go away," she said hoarsely. Then she sat down at one of the round tables and rested her face on her hands.

Ariadne still stood at the counter, uncertain what to do, her ice cream melting down between her fingers. When she saw that Mrs. Harrison's shoulders were shaking, she decided she'd better leave. But as she headed for the door, Mrs. Harrison said something.

"You can come up to me, but not down to me," she murmured. "That's what you said. And I tried—oh, May, I tried. But I couldn't find you." She rocked in her seat and gave a strangled sob.

"What?" Ariadne said. But Mrs. Harrison shook her head.

"Get out," she said. "We're closed."

Ariadne let herself out the door and saw Mrs. Harrison reach up and turn the lock. She looked at the cone in her hand. Yuck, she thought. I can't eat it now. She threw it into the garbage can on the corner and got back on her bike. Her legs were trembling, so she pedaled home slowly.

Now what? she thought. What am I supposed to do now?

She let herself into the house. Zephyr barreled out past her as she opened the door, and she stood in the hallway, gathering her thoughts.

No one was home but her dad. The MAN AT WORK— KEEP OUT sign hung crookedly on the closed study door. Fine. What could she say to him, anyway?

She threw herself on the big chair in the den, draping her legs over its arm, and went through the possibilities in her mind.

First: The other kids were playing a trick on her. No. She had to admit that that theory didn't work. How could they know what she was doing her report on? And besides, they just didn't seem like the type.

Second: She was going crazy. She turned that thought over slowly. She had heard that some kinds of mental illness started in your teens, and she would be thirteen in just two months. She saw someone that nobody else saw, and she heard voices. But if she was crazy, how did she see May Butler and hear her name before she ever read about her in that book? And anyway, her parents would have dragged her to a doctor if she had done anything weird, and she didn't think you could be crazy enough to see and hear people that didn't exist without acting at least a little strange in some other way.

Third: May Butler was a ghost. She had become a ghost in the nineteenth century, and she was still a ghost now. But that was ridiculous. There were no ghosts.

Or were there?

Ariadne was quiet at dinner, but no one noticed, of course. Hector was yammering about some kid in his class who had diabetes and had to stick his finger four times a day, and then their dad went on and on and *on* about his screenplay and how hard it was to write about people he wouldn't like if he met them on the street, and their mom talked about this article she read that really revolutionized the field of Greek epigraphy, whatever that was. It was driving her crazy. No, not crazy—she was just frustrated.

Ariadne pushed back her chair abruptly.

"May I please be excused?" she asked.

Her mother looked at her in surprise. "Aren't you hungry, sweetie?" she asked.

"No," she said, and fled before anyone could ask her any more questions. She just had to get out of there and do something to make her mind shut up about ghosts.

At least the computer was free now. She logged on and decided not to check her e-mail until she was about to log off. Save the best—a message from Sarah—for last. Ariadne moved the mouse around the pad that had a picture of her and Hector in their pajamas two Christmases ago, at home in Florida.

She went back to the page about the lake that she had bookmarked. She leaned close to the screen and looked hard at all the old pictures. The girls in front of the schoolhouse were wearing long dresses that looked a lot like May's. They were standing uncomfortably, bare toes flat against dirt that looked dry and dusty, and was now mud, with fish swimming in and out of the schoolhouse, in and out of the bell whose rope the teacher was clutching. Ariadne shivered. Did the old schoolhouse bell still ring too? Or was it just the church bell?

Those grim faces were giving her the creeps, so she went to the home page of Taylor County Public Schools. As it loaded, she thought how much things had changed. It wasn't as if a lot of time had passed since the picture of the barefoot children was taken. Some of the kids in front of the old school were probably still alive when the modern one was built. A photograph of the modern high school appeared, a big plain brick building with practically no windows. She clicked around and found a picture of some cheerleaders. Mostly blonde, tall, with naked legs and huge grins. The girls in the old school were pasty-faced, with hair bound back tight, everything but their faces and hands covered by clothes, squinting into the sun. They all looked like their names were Maude or Bertha or Clarabelle or something.

What a contrast with the modern picture! The caption gave their names. "Tiffany Benson," she read. "Jennifer Sloane, Leslie Kennedy—"

Leslie Kennedy? Her face looked familiar. Ariadne enlarged the picture and leaned back in her chair a little. That was Jade, wasn't it? Caroline's big sister? Unless there was a third Kennedy sister she hadn't met. But this obviously was Jade, although the picture was a year or two old, and in it she didn't look as curvy and tall as she was now. And Caroline had said something about Jade changing her name when she decided to become a model.

And May had said that she had two friends, Ann and Leslie. With a shiver, Ariadne heard Mrs. Unser's voice say, "Ann Fender got married years ago, and her married name is Harrison." Mrs. Harrison was Ann. Jade was Leslie. Ann and Leslie. She leaned her elbows on the computer table and stared at the screen.

"What are you doing?"

She spun around as her heart leaped wildly in her chest. "Jesus, Heck!"

"You're not supposed to say that," he said primly.

She stood up and grabbed him by the back of the neck, turning him around and marching him to the door as he squirmed and tried to beat her hand away.

"And you're not supposed to follow me around and sneak up on me and scare me like that!" she said.

"I scared you?" he said. "Hey, I'm good!" She could tell he was trying not to let on how much her grip hurt.

She shook him, pinching the back of his neck harder.

"Ow!" he cried.

"Addy!" her father called up the stairs. "Stop killing your brother!"

"I wish I *could* kill him!" she shouted. "He keeps following me around! Tell him to leave me alone!"

"I was not following her around," Hector said, and he started to cry as he broke free of her grip. "This is my house too. I can go to the study if I want to."

"Ariadne," their mother said, coming up the stairs. "What's gotten into you? I don't care what he did, you can't hurt him like that."

"And she said 'Jesus' when she was mad at me," said Hector, the tears stopping as quickly as they had started. "She's *crazy*."

"Shut up," Ariadne snarled. "I'm not crazy!"

"Stop it, both of you," their mother said. "Hector, go to your room and do your homework. Ariadne, log off this instant and go to your room. No more computer today."

"But Mom—" Ariadne began.

"I mean it," her mother said. "And if you talk back anymore, you won't get any computer time tomorrow."

"But—" Ariadne began again, but her mother held up a warning finger, and Ariadne knew she had to stop, or else. She could check her e-mail at school first thing in the morning, if she was really quick about it.

She stomped out of the room and slammed the door. It didn't make a loud enough bang, so she kicked it and felt satisfied when the smack that followed produced a shout from her father.

"You break that door, you pay for it, young lady!" he said.

"Gladly," she called back, and waited for his answer. But none came.

She threw herself on the bed. It was totally unfair. Not only did she have this whole May thing to worry about, but Hector wasn't giving her any privacy and her parents were taking his side. No more computer? She didn't even know if Sarah had written to her. And she couldn't check into May Butler's story anymore without a computer.

She'd just have to puzzle it out. Her father sometimes said that Sherlock Holmes's theory was that once you had eliminated the impossible, whatever is left, however improbable, must be the truth. She had already eliminated the practical-joke theory, and despite what Hector said, she knew she wasn't crazy.

So there was just one possibility left. And she refused to accept it. May *couldn't* be a ghost. First of all, only little kids believed in them. Second, May was so real. She was solid, and she had scraped that stinger out of Ariadne's finger and made her a mudpack.

Ariadne squirmed as she remembered May's touch. Her hand was ice cold and left a numb spot. But don't some people have cold hands? And maybe the numbness was because of some effect of the bee sting.

She was stifling, and not because it was hot—the air-conditioning made it comfortable—but because she was in a little bedroom in a small town in the middle of Tennessee. She was going to go nuts if she didn't get out. She had to stop thinking about May and get some fresh air into her.

The days were starting to get shorter, but it was still light out. She waited until she heard the TV—she knew her parents would be in the den watching some rerun or other—and she slipped down the stairs and out the door.

It had cooled off a lot since the early afternoon. The air smelled heavy and damp and kind of musty. Her dad said that no one had ever known such a rainy summer, and everything was soggy. That meant there was a lot of smelly mold and also a lot of bugs.

She made her way down to the lake. The sun was setting behind her, and the sky had a faint pink glow to it. From across the water she heard the sound of laughter and a car engine. Then nothing. She leaned back.

It must have been just like this in the days before the dam, she thought. Quiet, with lots of lightning bugs and—she slapped her cheek—mosquitoes. The only difference was the lake. The people in those days had a river, and they walked along it barefoot, like those kids in the picture. Or in heavy boots, like May.

What did all that stuff mean? Cold in summer, warm in winter. And then what Mrs. Harrison had said, "You can come up to me, but not down to me."

Maybe Ariadne's parents could figure it out. "Hi Mom, hi Dad, sorry I tried to kill jerkface Hector, I'll never do it again, and oh, by the way, what do you think it means if a strange girl dressed up like *Little House on the Prairie* tells you she's where it's cold in summer and warm in winter, and the cranky ice-cream lady tells you that you can go up to her but not down to her?"

The men in the white coats would be after her in an instant, and she would be locked away in some insane asylum until her hair turned as gray as Mrs. Harrison's. No, she couldn't tell anyone about May. There was no one she could trust. If only Sarah were here. But she wasn't, and this was the kind of thing that someone had to hear first-hand to believe or understand. On e-mail, it would just seem like a joke. And she needed to tell someone about May, someone who would see what it was that Ariadne was missing—the piece of the puzzle that would make it all make sense, if only she could find it. Because she refused to accept the only explanation that she could come up with—that May was a ghost.

The TV was turned off. Her dad opened the door to let Zephyr out for his evening run. He came sniffling up to her, wiggling happily. He curled up next to her and put his hot head on her lap.

But she didn't mind the extra heat. At least Zephyr had come and found her. Someone noticed she was out there and came to keep her company. She put her hand on his head and scratched where he liked, between the ears. He grunted contentedly.

No one else came to look for her. No one wondered where she was. A part of her knew they must have assumed she had gone to bed, but another part of her insisted that they knew she was gone and just didn't care where she was. She put her hands behind her head and leaned back, look-ing up at the fireflies, which were as thick as the stars. Why did they light only when they went up? A whole bunch of them would glow as they ascended and then go out before they started going down.

And why was their light so bright, without being hot?

She held one, and it felt positively cold as it crawled over her fingers. She caught her breath.

The firefly's light was cold in summer, and they lit only when they went up. Could this be a clue?

She shook her head. You're obsessing about this, she told herself sternly. Fireflies aren't warm in winter—they're dead in winter. And you don't go up to fireflies—they fly up. And what would it mean, anyway—that May had been reincarnated as a firefly? No, she was obviously on the wrong track here.

She should probably go inside before her father called Zephyr back in and locked the door. But it was so peaceful, with the fireflies and the silence and all. She felt herself growing drowsy, and as she dozed under the darkening sky, it seemed to her that the sound of a church bell, muffled by dozens of years and hundreds of feet of water, came drifting up to her from the dead town at the bottom of the cold, still lake.

fourteen

Ariadne biked home slowly, her head buzzing with sleepiness. It hadn't been a great day. She hadn't slept enough the night before—sometime before morning her mother had realized she wasn't in her room and had gotten hysterical thinking she had run away and then had really lost it when they found her sleeping in the grass. Hector had slept through it all, but somehow he had found out about it and teased her unmercifully all through breakfast, which came far too soon. Her parents glowered at her, and they didn't even try to stop him. When it was time for church, her mom wouldn't let her stay home. She rode her bike so she wouldn't have to talk to them.

And then church had been really dull, mostly because she could hardly keep her eyes open. She never thought she'd stay awake until the end of the service.

And it turned out that the mosquitoes and the fireflies weren't the only bugs out at night. She was covered in miserably itchy chigger bites. Why do they only get you in places you can't scratch in public? Ariadne thought, scratching the only bite that had appeared in a semi-decent place, her navel.

She crested the hill of the small town. It was so hot, and she was so tired. Maybe she'd get some ice cream and hope to get a burst of sugar-energy that would last her until she got home. But Fender's was closed. So she leaned her bike against the wall of the diner and went inside and ordered some fries and a Coke to go. She'd eat them on the little bench in the shade outside and then go home.

As she paid for her food, she heard a voice behind her call out, "Young lady!" and she turned to see Mr. Frank sitting at a table with two other old men. From the looks of the dirty dishes and empty coffee cups in front of them, they had just finished lunch.

She waved at him and then turned back to collect her change. She was glad that he didn't seem upset with her anymore.

She felt a tap on her shoulder. It was one of the other old men from Mr. Frank's table.

"Care to join us?" he asked. "Mack tells us you're going to make him a celebrity." Although Ariadne really didn't feel much like sitting with them, she didn't know how to say no, so she gathered her snack and sat down at the empty chair at the square Formica table. She unwrapped her fries.

"This is the little girl I was telling you about," Mr. Frank said. Ariadne saw a smear of ketchup on his cheek and had to resist the impulse to wipe it off. "She's going to write a paper about me and make me famous."

"La-di-*da*," said one of the old men.

"Is that true?" said the one opposite Ariadne. Like the other two, he had removed his cap, and his bald head was covered with dark spots, like big freckles. "What's so special about old Mack?"

But before she could answer, the other old man, whose thin face bore some silvery stubble around the chin and cheeks, said, "Vance here is the one you should be writing about. He's the one with the most interesting life." The other men laughed again. Goodness, they were certainly happy for a bunch of old guys, she thought.

She carefully chewed and swallowed before answering. "It's not really *about* Mr. Frank," she said. "It's about what life was like in the valley before they flooded it."

"See?" said Mr. Frank. "Vance didn't move here until after the dam was built. It don't matter how interesting his life has been—" The other two men laughed again, and Mr. Frank shot them the same glare he had given his daughter, but it didn't have the same effect. They kept chuckling and shaking their heads.

Mr. Frank ignored them and went back to Ariadne, "—so they wouldn't be any help at all."

The whiskery man stopped laughing and said, "*I* would, Mack. I've lived here all my life, at least so far, same as you. So you just ask me anything you want, young lady."

Oh, great. She was still sleepy and took a big swallow of the Coke to clear her head. It didn't help. What could she ask him? Not about May Butler, that was for sure. She didn't want to risk all of them getting weird on her, the way Mr. Frank did that last time.

They were looking at her expectantly.

"Um, what did you do for fun when you were kids?" she finally asked. "I mean, I know there wasn't any TV or radio or anything."

"We didn't have much time for fun," the whiskery man said. "After school, there were chores to do."

"Before school too," Mr. Frank said.

"Before too," agreed the other man. "But sometimes we'd have a few hours and we'd go running out in the woods. There were a lot more trees then, and the hills looked different somehow."

"What did you do in the woods?"

"Oh, we'd sometimes shoot a squirrel or a coon for stew," he said. "Or in the winter we'd build a fire and swap stories around it."

Ariadne almost asked what kind of stories, but it occurred to her that someone might bring up May Butler, and Mr. Frank would get upset again. He was a nice old guy, and she didn't want that to happen.

"What else?" she asked.

"Oh, we'd tell riddles and sing songs and such," he went on. "And sometimes—" He chuckled.

"Sometimes what?" Ariadne asked.

The old man looked at the other two as though asking for permission. They grinned at him.

"Sometimes," he said, "we'd go looking for stills. You know what a still is?"

"You mean like for making moonshine?"

"Exactly," he said, approvingly. "Some of our daddies and uncles earned good money out of those stills. They had to hide them from the police, but there wasn't much you could hide from a boy who knew these hills. We could tell you where every still was, and every lovers' lane, and every hollow tree, and every cave. We even found some Indian arrowheads in a cave once."

"You ever been in a cave?" asked the other old man.

Ariadne shook her head. "I've never even seen a hole that looked like it could be the entrance to one."

Mr. Frank said, "You can't usually see them. Sometimes they're all covered up with brush, and sometimes there's a big old rock hiding the mouth."

"So how do you find them if you can't see them?"

"Oh, you feel 'em."

"Feel them?"

"That's right," he said. "They're so big that they make their own weather. You can feel a breeze coming out of them. And since they're underground, the temperature is always the same inside, winter and summer. If you're in the woods and a wind blows on you that's cold in summer and warm in winter, you'll know you're standing by the mouth of a cave."

Ariadne felt as if she had fallen down one of the sink-holes Mrs. Unser had talked about. She put down her empty paper cup.

"What's the matter, honey?" Mr. Frank asked anxiously. "You don't look too good."

Ariadne did feel sick to her stomach. "I think I rode here too fast," she said. "I got hot on my bike, and it's so cool in here." She pressed her hands on her shorts to hide their trembling.

"You just sit still and let me get you a glass of water," Mr. Frank said. "Ed, quit talking to the little girl about caves. Can't you tell it bothers her?"

"Is that right?" the old man said as Mr. Frank went for the water, swinging his walker wide as he navigated around the shiny tables. "Do caves bother you? Some people purely can't stand them. Me, I always liked them."

"I don't know," Ariadne said. "I told you I've never been in one." Her voice sounded sharp, and she hoped the men wouldn't hear it.

Mr. Frank reappeared. "Janie's bringing some water," he said. "You're looking a little better now."

Ariadne nodded and took the glass of ice-cold water from the waitress, who stood looking down at her anxiously.

"You all right, hon?" she asked, and put her hand on

Ariadne's forehead. "You want me to call your mama to come pick you up?"

Ariadne shook her head and put down the glass. "I'm okay," she said. "Just tired and hot. I think I'll go home now."

"Just sit a few more minutes," said the waitress. "You boys keep an eye on her, hear?" And she went back behind the counter.

Ariadne pushed back her chair.

"I'm going to go home. It's all downhill. I'll be fine," she said as they chorused that she should sit there a little longer, that they would give her a ride home. I'm better off on my bike than in a car with one of them driving it, she thought.

"No, really," she said. "I can do it. Thanks a lot for talking to me."

And despite their protests, she made her way outside and hopped on her bike. She pumped a little to get started, and then leaned back in the bike saddle and coasted.

In a few minutes she was passing Caroline's house. Almost without planning to, she turned her bike and halted in front of the porch. I won't be able to stop thinking about it until I talk to Jade, she thought. She leaned her bike up against the porch rail and knocked on the screen door. No answer. She pushed the door open and poked her head in. "Hello?" she called. There were no cars in the driveway, so the parents were gone. Maybe the whole family had gone out. But just then Jade emerged from the den and saw Ariadne.

"The dork's out," she said, and kept walking.

"I wanted to see *you*," Ariadne said.

The ice goddess stopped and turned to stare at her with those leaf-green eyes. "Me?" Jade asked. "Why?"

Ariadne took a step closer. "I need to ask you something."

Jade shrugged her shoulders. "Okay," she said. "What is it?"

Ariadne took a deep breath. There had to be some explanation for that note of fear in Jade's voice when Caroline had asked her about May, and she wasn't going to be able to rest until she found out why. But she couldn't ask straight out.

"It's about my social-studies project," she said. "I'm researching how folktales got lost once there was radio and TV and stuff." Jade looked totally bored. "I know you grew up here, and I just wanted to ask you if you've ever heard a certain story."

"What story?" Jade said, shooting an impatient look toward the den, where the sound of the TV seemed to indicate that the commercial was over.

"A story about a girl who got lost," she said. "A girl named May Butler."

Jade froze, her hand on the doorknob. She licked her lips and said in a hoarse voice, just above a whisper, "What did you say?"

So she was right. Jade knew about May Butler, and she

wasn't just playing some stupid game. Her green eyes were wide open, and her face was white.

"I said, did you ever hear about a girl named May Butler?" When Jade didn't answer, Ariadne added, "And is your name really Leslie?"

"What?" Jade said, and then she shook her head as though to clear it. "Right, Leslie, that's my real name. But why are you asking me about May Butler?"

"She said you're a friend of hers," Ariadne said. "She said you were sick and she was worried about you." She was watching Jade, or Leslie, for a reaction, but the older girl looked frozen. "And she also said she's lost and wants me to find her, but I don't know where to look. Mrs. Harrison"—Jade stiffened—"Mrs. Harrison seems to know something about her."

Jade let go of the doorknob and leaned against the wall. She slid down until she was sitting on the floor, knees up by her chest. "So it's true," she said. "You've seen her too. I thought you had. I was hoping she was just a dream."

Ariadne stared at her, frozen.

"If she wasn't a dream, and you've seen her, then she's still lost." Jade put her face down on her knees. Her voice was muffled. "You have to help her. I tried, but I couldn't find her. And now I can't see her anymore. You have to do it. You have to find May Butler and take her home."

fifteen

Ariadne still couldn't say anything. None of it made any sense.

Jade lifted her head. "I was starting to think that I was crazy and I just imagined her."

"How did you meet her?" Ariadne finally asked.

"She used to come to me whenever I was home from the hospital. I was sick, did Caroline tell you?" Ariadne nodded. "I used to wish she would come while I was *in* the hospital, but she said she couldn't go that far from her momma. My friends acted like they were scared they'd catch leukemia from me, and they never visited, and Carrie was just a little kid. She was so afraid I would die that she couldn't talk about it. She'd run away whenever I went near her. My parents were busy pretending nothing was wrong. So when May came and acted like she wanted to talk to me, and then she listened while I told her everything that was happening . . ." Jade paused. "Well, she just about saved my life. I wish I could have found her.

But if you've seen her, I guess she's still lost." She hugged her knees.

Ariadne sat down next to Jade. She reached out a tentative hand and touched the older girl's shoulder. Jade didn't pull away.

"Maybe we can still find her," Ariadne said. "She told me that she was in a place where it's cold in summer and warm in winter. And Mrs. Harrison said you can go up to her, but not down. Is that what she told you?"

Jade raised her head, looking bewildered. "No," she said, "but what she told me doesn't make any more sense than what she told you and Mrs. Harrison."

"What did she say?" Oh please, thought Ariadne, let it be a clue that leads me somewhere.

"She said to look for her under the bear."

Ariadne slumped, defeated.

"Great," she said. "That makes about as much sense as going up a chimney down but not down a chimney up."

"What?" Jade said.

"Nothing," Ariadne said. She would never find May Butler now.

"Anyway, so I went out to the bear and looked under it—"

"*What?*" Ariadne said. "You looked for her under a bear? What bear?" This conversation was getting weirder by the minute.

"That's what people who used to live in the valley call that big knob of rock at the point," Jade said. "You know, where the road ends. I went out there, I don't know how many times, and looked around the bear, under the overhangs, everything. I even brought a shovel and tried to dig, but the ground is solid rock. There's nothing under the bear. Nothing."

Ariadne felt a chill. "Tried to dig?" she said. "But how could you find someone under the ground?" No, she thought. No, no, no. Don't say it.

"You could if they were dead," she said.

"Are you trying to tell me that May Butler is—"

"A ghost," Jade said.

"A *ghost*?" Ariadne gasped. "But she touched me, and her hand was solid." She stopped, remembering the icy feeling that touch had left. She cleared her throat and went on. "And she took a bee stinger—"

"So what?" Jade said impatiently. "Do you think that ghosts go through things, like in the movies? Maybe some do, but not May. She couldn't help people if she couldn't touch them. And she has to help people."

Ariadne didn't know what to say. It was the weirdest thing she had ever heard, but it had the ring of truth to it. Thinking about it, she had to admit that she had known it for a while. She had just refused to accept it. But now, hearing those words in Jade's matter-of-fact voice, it made so much sense that she couldn't argue against it anymore.

Jade said with a kind of big-sister superiority, "Don't think you and I are the only ones who've seen her. Other people have."

"Like Ann Fender?" Ariadne asked.

"Yes, Mrs. Harrison," Jade said. "And there was an old man who lived here. Mr. Archer. He had polio or something. He could hardly walk and was all crooked. My mom said that people avoided him when he was younger. One day he just started to talk to me. He told me he knew I had seen May."

"Where is he now?"

"He died," Jade said. "But I knew what he meant. When I met you, I could tell you had seen her too. I don't know how, but I knew. And I didn't want to believe it. But then you started hanging out with Carrie—" She shook her head and sighed. "Well, I knew there was no way I could keep avoiding you. So I tried not to think about it."

"Why didn't you want to know I had seen her?"

"I told you," Jade said, and her voice had regained some of its ice-princess edge. "I was hoping she would turn out to be a dream. Because if she wasn't a dream, then I was probably nuts. And if I wasn't crazy, then I had failed her. I couldn't help her, when she'd helped me so much.

"I was tired of being the one that everyone had to help. Poor, sick Leslie," she said bitterly, in a mocking tone. "Poor girl, she never was a real beauty, but she did have that pretty hair, and now it's all gone and she looks like a duck egg. Everybody, be nice to Leslie. And they were," she went on in her normal voice. "They invited me places and sat next to me at school. But they didn't really want to. They were just doing it because they thought it would be mean not to."

Ariadne nodded. That sure sounded familiar.

"But when May helped me it was different. She just listened, and she didn't stare at my bald head, but she didn't look away from it either. She just acted like I was normal. So when I had a chance to help *her*, it made me so happy." Her voice quivered at these last words, and she scrubbed at her nose with the back of her hand. "But it was no use. I couldn't help her. I couldn't help anybody."

And then she stood up, walked into the other room, and closed the door. Ariadne heard the sound of a lock being turned.

Ariadne felt chilled, but she knew that what Jade—Leslie—said was true. Her mind had refused to believe the only real explanation: the girl she had seen and talked to, the girl who had removed a bee stinger from her finger, the girl with the sad face and the gentle voice, was dead. A ghost.

In a strange way, Ariadne felt relieved. May *was* real—if you can call a ghost "real"—and someone else had seen her. Lots of people, if Jade was right. So Ariadne wasn't crazy or being picked on by girls she had thought might turn into friends.

Now there was a new problem. She was supposed to find May and somehow help her get home. It's hopeless, Ariadne thought as she coasted down the hill between Caroline's house and her own. She didn't know where to look, and she didn't even really know what she was looking for. And how do you help a ghost go home, anyway? Where do ghosts live?

She rode into their driveway. No car, so Dad must have gone out, and her mother wouldn't be home until dinnertime. She went to the kitchen in search of something to eat. There was an open bag of chips on the floor, but it was empty. Licked clean, in fact. And under the kitchen table was Zephyr, wagging his fat body with a guilty look on his face.

"Did you eat all my chips, you bad boy?" she asked, and bent over to kiss his nose. He licked her face. "Don't you know you're supposed to be on a doggie diet? And who left them where you could get them?" She picked up the bag to use as evidence and walked out of the kitchen.

"Hector!" she called. No answer. She poked her head up the stairwell. "Heck! Did you leave the chips where Zephyr could get them?"

"Shut up!" came a voice from upstairs. Terrific. That was all she needed, a cranky little brother. But he owed her for letting Zephyr get at the chips, so she went up the stairs two at a time. She knew better than to enter his room when he was in that kind of mood, but he had left his door open, and she was within her rights to stand in the doorway. It was part of the hallway, after all.

"Thanks a lot—" she started indignantly, and then stopped. Hector was sitting cross-legged on his bed, and he obviously had been crying. His face was streaked with tears, and his nose was running. Not a pretty sight.

"What's the matter, Heck?" she asked. She dared to take a step in the door. He didn't chase her out, so she went all the way in and sat down next to him. She pulled a tissue out of the box on his bedside table and passed it to him. "You have snot all over your face," she said, as he blew his nose. He didn't answer, and he didn't try to gross her out. Wow. He must really feel bad.

"So what's up?" she asked. His lower lip was quivering.

"Did you get hurt?" she asked. "Did you fall off your bike?" He shook his head. "So what is it?"

"It's that *jerk,*" he said raggedly. "That butt-head Bruce."

"What did he do?" she asked.

"He told everybody that I was a sucky fisher and that Dad is a wimp because he won't let me have a gun and that he was only being friendly with me because he was sorry for me, but I was so mean he wasn't going to hang out with me anymore. And I *wasn't* mean to him. I've been as nice as I could be, and I thought he was my friend."

"He's a toad," Ariadne said. "A dork. Forget him. You can make new friends."

"Oh yeah?" he said. "That's not what you've been saying ever since we came here. All you talk about is Sarah and how much better everything was in Florida. Those other girls were nice to you, and you don't call them up or anything. So don't tell *me* I can make new friends."

"All right, all right," Ariadne said. He was obviously in no mood to be consoled, so she went back downstairs.

None of this was getting her any closer to finding May. What on earth could all those things mean? Cold in summer, warm in winter; under the bear; can go up to her but not down. Maybe there was another bear? But no, Jade grew up here and would know. She had to be in a cave. But how could there be a cave under the bear?

There was a note on the counter.

"Addy/Heck," it read, like they were one person. "Dad and I got invited to a cocktail party, so you're on your own for dinner. There's some frozen pizza, and you can each have one—ONE!—Coke. I counted them, so I'll know. I have my cell phone, so call me if you need me."

Ariadne checked out the freezer. Two big pizzas, hers with extra cheese, and Heck's with every kind of greasy meat known to man. Even though it was still early, she turned on the oven, and when Hector smelled the pizzas cooking, he came thundering down the stairs. He had blown his nose and washed his face, but he was obviously still trying his best to keep a dignified silence.

Ariadne took this as a challenge. She spread newspaper on the floor of the den, and they ate and drank their one Coke each while they watched TV, even though their mom would kill them if she found out. Hector hogged the best spot and stared at the screen, giving one-word answers to her questions, until she went to the kitchen and pulled two more Cokes out of her hidden stash in the back of the cupboard where their parents kept the utensils they rarely used.

She returned to the den with her hands behind her back and stood in front of the TV until Hector was forced to say, "*Move,* Ariadne," and she triumphantly showed him the Cokes. His face lit up, just as she knew it would, and he moved over to give her room on his cushion. They drank the warm Cokes and ate the rest of the pizzas, giving the crusts to Zephyr. He was so thrilled to be cheating on his diet that he nearly took their fingers off when he grabbed the treats.

Ariadne didn't say anything when Hector turned on one of those real-life cop shows she knew their father would never let him watch, but sat with him for a while and joined in when he heaped scorn on the heads of the would-be criminals who always seemed to wind up flat on their big bellies in the dirt, their faces turned into blurs by television magic, their hands cuffed behind them.

But after the third or fourth time the cop said, "You can

run, but you can't hide," she became bored and stepped out onto the porch.

It was nice out. Still light, and warm, but with a little edge to the heat that warned that pretty soon it would be getting cool. She had never spent more than a weekend in a cold place and wondered if it ever snowed in Tennessee.

She walked out to the end of their boat dock. Her father had had to pull the land end of it higher up onto the shore yesterday. He said it had been such a wet summer that the lake was at the highest level it could possibly go without spilling over the dam. No one could remember the last time it had been that high. From the dock she could see the point of land sticking into the water, and the rock on top that did look just like a big old bear sitting back on its haunches. It was at the very end of the point, which dropped off in a sheer cliff straight to the water, so the bear looked as if it were surveying the lake.

You can come up to me, but not down to me, she thought silently. Look for me under the bear.

Jade thought that meant May was *buried* under the bear. But what if she meant that she was at the bottom of the cliff under the bear? Straight down?

Ariadne's dad had said that the water was a hundred feet deep there. She'd never be able to find anything under it.

She just had to get out on the lake. She couldn't wait for

her father to get home so they could go out in the rowboat. She'd think of some reason. A father-daughter talk—he'd love that one. And once they were out, she'd find an excuse to row under the bear. There had to be some kind of clue— there just had to be. And then she could come back later without her dad and do whatever it was May wanted her to do.

Ariadne walked halfway up the hill to the house and listened. No car. Back down at the dock, she looked up at the bear again. The air had an even cooler edge to it. If her father didn't come soon, she'd have to wait until tomorrow, or maybe even longer, and she couldn't stand that.

She looked back at the house and hesitated. Hector wouldn't notice she was gone until the last TV criminal was pushed into a squad car. But if she got caught out on the lake without an adult, she'd be grounded until she was forty. No big loss, she thought. Grounded from doing what? It's not like I'm being swamped with invitations that I'd have to turn down. She looked at the wooden rowboat. It was almost new, and solid. No holes or cracks or anything like that. The water was perfectly still. She stepped into the boat, then hesitated again. Should she be leaving Hector alone? But her dad had been going on and on about how safe it was here. Surely he wouldn't do anything stupid in the short time it would take her to go check out the bear. So she buckled on a life jacket and started rowing.

She kept close to the shore. One eye caught a flash of movement in the woods, and she turned her head quickly, but whatever it was had gone. Just a squirrel or a raccoon, she thought. But the flash had looked blue. Optical illusion, she told herself firmly, and she kept rowing. She heard some jet-skis buzzing behind her, but mostly the lake was empty.

Ariadne approached the point. Funny—from far away, the edge of the cliff had looked so sharp, like a knife-edge rising out of the water, but when you got close, it was a broad piece of rock. She dropped the oars and rubbed her sore hands together, looking down at the water. If it was as deep here as her dad said, May was right about not being able to go down to her. You sure couldn't get to the bottom of the lake without scuba-diving equipment. But how could you go *up* to someone who was at the bottom of a lake?

She stared at the water, feeling a little foolish. What was she looking for, anyway? A sign saying MAY BUTLER LIES HERE? A ghostly face floating up through the water?

The thought made her shudder, as though an icy wind had blown down her back. Then she froze. The icy wind was not just fear—it was an actual cold breeze. And this was summer.

Ariadne looked up at the side of the cliff. There was no opening in it that she could see. But then *where* was the wind coming from? Gently, so as not to disturb the faint air current, she turned the boat. No, now it was gone. She turned back and felt the breeze a little bit, then rowed a stroke and lost it again. She rowed, drifted, turned again, until the bow of the rowboat nuzzled up against the cliff. And the cool wind was now so strong that it was making her hair blow gently back from her cheeks.

She grabbed hold of some weeds to keep from drifting and chewed her lip, staring at the nearly sheer wall. Maybe she should go home and tell her parents what she had found. Sure. "Hi, Mom and Dad, how was your day? Can we go look for a ghost who told me she's in a cave?" No, she was on her own.

She craned her neck to look up the cliff again. She still didn't see an opening, but from this angle the rock was so bumpy and irregular that any outcropping of stone could hide one. It was really, really steep. In fact, parts of it curved out and hung over her.

A cloud passed behind the cliff, and she clutched the sides of the boat, feeling a moment of vertigo, like the whole mountain was about to fall on her. If May was here someplace, and not underwater, it was easy to see why she had told Mrs. Harrison that you couldn't get down to her. Only an expert rock climber could make it down that sheer drop from the top, where the bear crouched overhead. But was she right about the first part? *Could* Ariadne get up to her?

She tied the boat to a scrubby tree that leaned out over the water and carefully stood up. The boat rocked underfoot, and she clutched the top branch of the little tree in panic. As soon as her heart quit pounding so hard, she placed her feet on bumps in the rock and climbed up a few feet. Another little tree was growing from a ledge right above her, and she found some footholds that raised her close enough to reach it. Holding on to the thin trunk to steady herself, she climbed up and stood on the ledge next to the tree. There was just room for both her feet, and the only solid thing to hold on to was a thin shelf of rock right above her shoulders. But the breeze was definitely stronger here, and it seemed to be coming straight out from the cliff face.

Her heart started pounding again as she slid her feet along the ledge. She found a place to put her right foot and hauled herself up a little. Then her left foot found a hole. This was easier than she thought. She climbed up a few more steps, then glanced back down over her left shoulder and instantly wished she hadn't. Had she really climbed that far?

But now her fingertips were wrapped around the edge of an opening, and the breeze flowing over them was very cool. If she could just haul herself up, maybe she could see something. I wish I had practiced chin-ups a little more in P.E., she thought. She gripped tighter and pulled. Her feet scrabbled against the rock of the cliff wall, and her toe managed to hit something. She tried not to think about losing her grip and sliding down into that endlessly deep water. She pulled to get up high enough to look into the place the breeze was coming from.

But she must have pulled too hard, or shoved too hard with her feet, because suddenly she flipped over the lip of the opening and fell headfirst, sliding on her belly down the gravelly wall of a cave. She thought of that sinkhole on the ridge road. I'll break every bone in my body! she thought, and screamed and tried to grab on to something.

At that instant she hit bottom. She lay there for a few seconds, breathing hard, then sat up and groaned. She would be coated with bruises, she was sure, only in the pitch dark of the cave it was impossible to see. She felt herself all over, and there didn't seem to be any blood. The life jacket must have protected her from getting too smashed up. Her trembling hands were scraped from grabbing at the wall and hitting the hard floor first.

She looked up, panting, and saw a crack of deep blue sky. It looked like it was a million miles away.

And then a chill seized her. Nobody knew she was there. Nobody would come looking for her. She would die in this cave. And nobody would ever know what had happened to her, just like no one ever knew what had happened to May Butler.

sixteen

Panic welled up, and she fought it down fiercely. Someone will see the boat, Ariadne told herself. They'll wonder what it's doing here and come to investigate. They'll find me. But then she realized that the little wooden rowboat blended in perfectly with the surroundings. Unless someone was right on top of it, they wouldn't see it. Who would think to look on the lake, anyway? No one knew she had gone out in the boat. It might be days before they noticed it was missing and realized she had taken it, and then it might be weeks or even months before anyone happened to spot it against the cliff.

And even if they did, would they find the cave? Its opening was so well hidden that she never would have thought to look there if she hadn't been following the cool breeze. And if whoever found the boat didn't pay attention to that little wind. . . . She shuddered. They could be right outside and never see the cave, and if she was asleep—or unconscious—when they came, she couldn't call out to them.

But maybe someone could hear her now. "Help!" she shouted, but the sound disappeared into the emptiness so spookily that she stopped. No one would be able to hear her unless they were right next to the opening.

Maybe she could climb out. She tried to figure out how high the cave wall was. She imagined standing on her dad's shoulders—how high could she reach? Picturing it, she figured that it was about ten feet to the opening. It went practically straight up. Her mouth felt dry. She could never climb that.

But she had to try. What choice did she have? Maybe there was something to grab hold of. She took off her life jacket and stood on it, feeling her way up the wall. Nothing. She moved sideways a little and tried again. Still nothing. She walked along the whole side, patting the wall. But it was smooth, except for the gravel that showered down as she groped around.

Maybe she should walk all the way around the cave. Perhaps it went back into the hill and came out somewhere. But the thought of exploring that blackness was more than she could handle. And anyway, what if the floor of the cave suddenly disappeared and she fell again, this time farther into the earth? She couldn't risk that. She'd rather die. No, not die! She wasn't going to die here.

She sat down on her life jacket and tried not to panic. Think, she said to herself. Pretend it's a math problem.

Ariadne is five feet, four inches tall. She is at the base of a smooth ten-foot wall. She is wearing summer clothes and has a pocket knife and a life jacket. How can she get to the top of the wall? Nothing came to her.

She paced, sat down, got up, paced again. Still nothing. She was getting thirsty. Just out of reach was a whole lake full of water. Full of a dead town and little brown fish and cow poop, but still water. She pushed the fear away. How long could she last without water? A few days? Surely someone would come before then. *Surely* they would.

The faint sounds of water lapping against the cliff made her thirst grow sharper. Maybe the water would rise even higher and fill the cave, and she could float out. Maybe . . . but it was no use. The water would never get that high. It was right at the top of the dam already, and if it got any higher it would just spill over the edge without raising the level of the lake at all, and without flooding the cave and floating her out.

She sat on the floor of the cave, her head on her knees. What will happen first? she wondered. Terrible thirst? Probably. And again she fought down panic. She had to keep her head clear and think of something to do. She wasn't going to just sit there and wait for it to happen.

Ariadne stood up and put one hand on the wall of the cave. The image of herself falling down a huge crack in the floor made her hesitate. I'll just move carefully, she thought, and slid one foot slowly after the other. The wall was lumpy and hard and rough, but she patted every inch of it as high as she could go.

Suddenly a little passageway opened up, and her heart jumped into her throat. Maybe all she had to do was walk down this a little way, and she'd get out. But as she slid her foot forward, she thought she felt a tug on her arm—not enough to make her lose her balance but so startling that she froze in her tracks.

Did a voice whisper "Careful" in her ear? She whipped around with outstretched arms, but there was nothing there. It must have been her imagination, or the wind. She swallowed hard and put her hand on her chest, where her heart seemed to be jerking around wildly. When she had caught her breath, she slid her right foot, more cautiously this time, along the floor.

And felt nothingness beneath it. She jumped back and clutched the outcropping of rock that her hand was resting on.

Calm down, she thought, and she cleared her throat and said it out loud. "Calm down, Ariadne," but her voice sounded so weird that she instantly regretted it.

Maybe it was just a little hole, she thought. Maybe she could climb down it and up the other side, and continue her exploration. She leaned backward and poked a toe down. She didn't feel anything. She lay on her belly and reached her hand down. Nothing. She picked up a pebble and dropped it.

Almost immediately she heard a soft splash. Of course, the hole would be full of water. It was probably right about at the level of the lake, and water would be seeping in. Maybe it was just a little underground lake and she could swim to the other side and find an opening—

No. She shuddered at the thought of swimming in the pitch darkness, not knowing where she was going, not knowing what little blind fish might live in the water, distant cousins of the ones that nibbled her feet in the lake. What if she started swimming, and the water went on and on, and she got turned around and confused, and she swam and swam and never found her way out again?

She couldn't do it.

But maybe the underground lake was small, and there was a way out on the other side of it. She crawled on her knees and one hand, her left hand running around the lip of the opening. She was right; it wasn't very big, but when she reached the other side, she felt a solid wall of rock.

She stood up and slowly and cautiously, once again sliding her feet along the bottom, worked her way back around to the spot where she had first landed.

So this is it, she thought. This is where I'm going to die. She felt strangely calm. She pictured her parents, wondering where she was, looking for her, hanging posters all over, getting a search party together. Like May's father, she thought.

She made a pillow out of her life jacket and curled up tightly. She would just lie there. Maybe she would lose consciousness before the hunger and thirst got too bad. If she listened hard enough, maybe she could hear the church bell, or even the school bell, from the drowned town. The thought comforted her in an odd way. She would die, but she wouldn't be alone. In the future, when the bells rang for the dead town, they'd be ringing for her too.

And then she did hear something. But it wasn't bells.

She lifted her head and held her breath. It was a buzz, and it was coming from outside the cave, on the lake. It sounded like—yes, it was a jet-ski. And it was getting louder. She leaped to her feet and screamed, "Help! Somebody help me! I'm stuck in a cave!" Even though she knew that the noise of the engine would drown out her voice, she couldn't stop screaming.

Miraculously, the jet-ski driver cut the engine. Maybe he could hear her now. "Help, oh, help!" she shouted, sobbing and jumping as high as she could to make her voice reach out of the cave. "Please help me!"

The cave opening was dim, since the overhang covered it almost completely. It suddenly got even darker. Was that someone's head blocking the light? Oh please, she thought again, and called, a sob breaking her voice, "Help me! I fell in this cave and I can't get out!"

"Ariadne?"

"*Hector?*" she cried in disbelief. "What are you doing here?"

"I wasn't following you," he said. "I really wasn't."

"It's okay," she said, her heart thumping. "It's okay if you followed me this time."

"But I didn't," he insisted. "You're not supposed to go out in the boat without a grown-up. And why did you go in this cave?"

"I didn't go here on purpose, you idiot," she said. Her knees were trembling so with relief that she had to lean against the cave wall. "I fell in."

"Like Alice in Wonderland," he said. "And I'm not an idiot."

"I'm sorry," she said, trying not to cry. "Just get me out, Heck."

"How?"

"I don't know," Ariadne said. A thought struck her. "Where'd you get the jet-ski? Ask the person you got it from—"

"I took it off the Parrishes' dock," he said.

"You *stole* it?"

"I borrowed it. There's nobody home over there, but I didn't think they'd mind. I couldn't get it started for a while, and then it was hard to steer, but I figured it out. Hey, I know what—I can get that rope myself. Be right back!"

"Hector, stop!" she called, but it was too late. The jet-ski engine kicked into life again, and faster than she would have thought possible, the sound died away.

That dope. She was going to tell him to call the Coast Guard, 911, anybody. Now she would have to rely on him to get a long-enough rope. And not drown on the way. But she had been found. Thank goodness, she had been found! No wonder May was so sad. If it was this awful to be lost for half an hour, she could understand why May felt so bad about being lost for more than one hundred years.

It seemed like forever before she heard the jet-ski again, but finally Hector's head appeared in the cave opening.

"Which rope did you bring?" she asked.

"That long yellow one," he answered, and disappeared again. Good; that was the one they took camping. It was made of nylon—her dad said it was impossible to break—and was yards and yards long. It would surely reach her.

"Tie it to something good and sturdy," Ariadne ordered him.

His head reappeared. "Hey, I'm the one who's saving your life, so quit the bossy stuff."

"Okay, okay," she said. It was a small price to pay. If Hector would just get her out, she'd never boss him again for the rest of her life. And she'd never fuss at him for following her again. She wanted him to keep talking, to remind her she wasn't alone anymore.

Hector appeared again.

"Who was that girl?" he asked.

"What girl?"

"That girl you sent to tell me to come here."

Ariadne's heart began to thump again. "I didn't send anyone," she said.

"Well, then who was she?"

"I don't know," Ariadne answered, although she thought she had a good idea. "What did she look like?"

"Kind of your age, but smaller, and her hair was in one of those things, you know, like a long ponytail, but twisted."

"A braid?"

"I guess so. And a golden necklace. And she told me that you needed me to go as fast as I could to the rock that looked like a bear. I think it looks like Zephyr, but I figured out what she meant."

"I don't know who she is," Ariadne said, although her legs were trembling again, and she had to lean against the wall and slide down until she was sitting. "She must have been someone who saw me fall in and figured that you could help." Pretty weak, but apparently Hector bought it, because he disappeared again without saying anything.

"How did you reach up to the cave mouth so easily?" she asked the next time his head darkened the small cave opening. If it was hard for her, it must have been a real stretch for someone six inches shorter.

"Cinchy," he said. "Those holes are just like steps. And then I just did a chin-up like in P.E."

"It figures," she muttered. The first practical use for anything anyone ever did in P.E. "Do you have that rope tied yet?"

"Do you want me to just tie one old granny knot that will come undone and drop you on your butt, or do you want me to do it right?"

"Okay," she said impatiently. "Do it right. Hey, did you bring a flashlight?"

"Yep," he said. "And I even put new batteries in it. And I left a note saying where we were. That's what took me so long. Why do Mom and Dad keep batteries in the refrigerator?"

She ignored his question. "Tie the flashlight to the end of the rope and lower it down," she said. "I want to see what's in here."

"Okay," came the answer, and in a few minutes the flashlight was sliding down the gravelly slope that had imprisoned her for what seemed like hours.

"Slower!" Ariadne called. "If you bump it, it might break!"

"What's there to see in there anyway?" Hector asked.

"It's creepy being in the dark," she said. "And anyway, I want to see how far back the cave goes."

Compared to what she had seen on the Discovery Channel, this was one dull cave. It was plain brown. She aimed the light at the floor toward the back of the cave, onto the water that she had almost fallen into. The underground pond was black and shiny. It wasn't very wide, she realized, but she'd been right that she wouldn't have gotten very far if she'd tried to swim it. Past the water, a solid wall of rock rose farther than the light of her flashlight would reach. She slowly played the flashlight around the rest of the cave.

No bat droppings streaked the walls, and there were no stalactites or stalagmites or old paintings of buffaloes or anything. It looked like no one had ever been in here.

But someone had. Or, at least, someone had dropped something in from the outside, because there was a shoe. Two shoes, in fact. They looked old and crumpled, but they were definitely shoes. They sat neatly side by side, as though someone had carefully put them there. She picked one up. It was strange; instead of laces, it had buttons running up the side. She put it down next to its mate and moved the light around the floor in a slow arc. It was very flat, almost like a floor in a house.

She stopped as the smooth surface gave way to a lumpy patch. "Oh no," she whispered. "No, please don't let it be . . ."

But it was. On the floor was something that looked like cloth. It lay in shreds, with a layer of dust covering it.

"Ariadne!" It was Hector. "Come pull on the rope and see if it's tied tight enough!"

She didn't answer. She couldn't. She knelt by the shreds of cloth and gently brushed at the dust, revealing a faded pattern of pale flowers on what looked like a blue background.

And that wasn't all. Inside the cloth was something long and hard and pale. She turned the flashlight directly on it, but she knew what it was even before the beam hit it.

"Ariadne!" Hector called. "The rope's ready! Come and pull on it."

"Okay," Ariadne said. "Just a minute."

She leaned over and blew the dust so that it flew up in a tiny cloud.

"Come on!" Hector called again. "What are you *doing* in there?"

But she couldn't tell him. Because what she was doing was looking at a skeleton. And she knew, as surely as she knew anything in this world, that it was May Butler's.

seventeen

"Ariadne!" Hector was still calling. "Let's get out of here! It's getting dark. And what if the Parrishes come home and see that their jet-ski's missing? They'll call the police and then we'll be in *big* trouble!"

But Ariadne couldn't take her eyes away from the bones. Oddly, they didn't scare her. How could gentle May Butler, dead or alive, scare anyone? Instead, they made her feel like crying. If May had been climbing up the cliff, exploring, or going after something, she could easily have slipped in, just as Ariadne had. Maybe she died quickly in the fall, she told herself. But the shoes said otherwise. May had lived long enough to take them off to try to get a toehold on the wall.

"Ariadne!" It was Hector again. "Come up right now or I'm going to leave you! Then Dad will have to come get you, and he'll be really, really mad!"

"Okay, okay!" Ariadne called back. "I'm coming!" If their dad saw the cave, he would think it was neat and would want to explore it. Somehow she knew that May wouldn't want everyone gawking at her bones. After all, she was choosy about who she showed herself to. Ariadne's parents would never understand. Her mother would call someone from the college, like an archaeologist, and there would be an article in the newspaper with pictures and everything. No, she would have to figure out herself what, if anything, to do with the bones.

But first she had to get herself out of there. She knew she could never climb the rope—she was hopeless at that in P.E. too—and Hector wasn't strong enough to pull her up. But as she tugged on the rope to make sure it was secured, she realized that Hector had already worked it out. He had tied loops every few feet in the rope.

"Stick one foot in a loop and pull yourself up, and then stick your other foot in the next loop," he said. "Just keep going like you're climbing a ladder."

"How did you know how to do that?" she asked. "Cub Scouts?"

"Nope," he said proudly. "Figured it out myself. Pretty good, huh?"

"Excellent," she said, and meant it. Hector wasn't such a dope after all. She cast a glance over her shoulder, reluctant to leave May after it had been so hard to find her. "I'll be back," she whispered. "I promise." Then she started to climb out.

But it wasn't quite as easy as Hector had made it sound. One of the loops came undone, so she had to really stretch to make the next one, and another was so tight that her foot got stuck in it, and she had to yank off the loop with one hand while clinging to the rope with the other and banging into the cave wall. When she finally hauled herself over the edge of the cave opening, her arms and legs were shaking from the exertion.

"Just a little more," Hector said. "Turn around and slide. Your feet are only a foot above the boat. Come on." It was oddly comforting to have her little brother tell her what to do in such a confident tone. So she did as he said, and suddenly there she was, slumped on the seat of the rowboat. She reached for the oars, but her arms were so rubbery that she knew she couldn't row. "Heck—" she started, but he was already tying the rowboat to the back of the jet-ski.

"The rope's pretty short, so you'll get bumped around some in my wake, but I'll go real slow," he promised. He turned on the motor, and they took off slowly. She held on tight to both sides of the boat and looked around. It was like seeing the lake for the first time. The ridges of the little waves, turned golden by the setting sun, were so beautiful that she felt sudden tears.

Hector took them back to the Parrishes' dock. He tied the jet-ski to its mooring, unhitched the rowboat, got into it, and picked up the oars to row the short distance to their own dock.

"You're facing the wrong way," Ariadne said.

"I am not," Hector said, flailing the oars around.

"You are too," Ariadne said.

"I was just trying a new way to row," Hector said. "Move over."

New way to row. Sure. But she didn't say anything, and they were finally making some progress toward their own dock. Hector jumped out and tied the boat to the cleat.

"Come on," he said. Ariadne hoisted herself off the seat painfully. She hadn't realized how much she had been banged up in her fall and then in the climb, but now she saw scrapes and bruises on her legs and arms. The palms of her hands were scraped and filthy.

"You look crummy," Hector said.

"Shut up and help me out," she said, reaching a hand toward him.

"Not if you tell me to shut up," he said, leaning away from her and putting his hand behind his back.

"Please, brother dear, please help me out of the boat." Her voice was wavering, so Hector took pity on her and hauled her up onto the dock. "Do you think Mom and Dad are back?" she asked, starting up the steep slope toward the house.

"I hope not," he said. "And you'd better hope not too, because if they are, you're in *big* trouble. You're not supposed to take the rowboat out by yourself."

"You said that already," she snapped. "And anyway, you took the jet-ski, and it's not even ours, and you didn't wear a life jacket."

"I saved your life by taking it! I'm a hero!"

"But you should have put on a life jacket!" she said.

"Okay," he said. "I won't tell if you don't."

"Deal," she said, and let herself in the back door. The house was dark and silent. What a relief. The light on the answering machine was flashing, but for once she didn't dive at it to see if it was a message from Sarah.

"Hector, throw out the note you left for Mom and Dad, and get the message off the answering machine," she said. "I need to take a shower."

"You sure do," he said, but she ignored him.

The hot water felt so good. She watched as the water at her feet turned muddy and then clear as the crusted dirt melted off her elbows, her knees, her shins. A twig that must have been in her hair swirled around the drain. As she toweled dry, she found herself worrying about May. Ariadne could probably get her bones out of the cave, but then what? May wanted to go home, but home was under a hundred feet of water. How would Ariadne ever figure out where it was and how to return May there?

A knock came at the door. "That was Mom on the answering machine," Hector said. "She said they were on their way back, and they'd be home at eight."

"What time is it now?" She was answered by the sound of the car crunching over the gravel of the driveway. "Remember, Heck, not a word about what happened," she said, but he was already thudding down the stairs. She hoped that he would be so afraid of their parents' anger at the unauthorized jet-ski ride, and especially without a life jacket, that he would keep his mouth shut. She dressed quickly and went downstairs.

There were her mother and father, in party clothes, talking and laughing about the people at the college president's house. They suddenly looked so nice, so whole, so real, that she gave them each a big hug.

"Hey, Addy!" Her father sounded pleased. "It's been a while since I got one of your squeezes."

"Mmm-mmm," said her mother, nuzzling her wet hair. "Not only a squeeze, but from a clean girl, no less." Her voice changed. "Sweetie—" she was looking at Ariadne's knees. "How on earth did you get so skinned up?"

"I fell," Ariadne said.

"Good thing you always wear your helmet," her father said. "Did you hurt yourself anyplace else?"

What a relief. They thought she was talking about her bike. She shot Hector a warning glance, and he rolled his eyes up to the ceiling, making an innocent face.

"I bumped my shoulder," she said, "and I have a few other bruises."

Her mother looked worried. "Maybe we should run you by the emergency room," she said.

"Oh no, Mom," she said. Maybe the doctor could somehow tell it wasn't a bike accident and would ask her questions she didn't want to answer. "I'm fine. Really."

"Really," Hector chimed in. "She's fine."

"Okay, you two, she's fine," their father said. "But make sure you keep those scrapes clean so they don't get infected."

"I will," Ariadne promised. "How was the party?" she asked, to change the subject. Her father shot her a quizzical glance, like he was wondering why she cared.

"It was fun," their mother said. "And we had so many appetizers that we don't need any dinner. But I feel like some dessert. Let's get an ice cream, okay?"

"Not ice cream," their father said. "I've been craving that chess pie at the Dobbin Diner."

"Why do they call it chess pie?" Hector asked. "It doesn't have squares on it."

"Because it's not apple pie, and not peach pie, and not pecan pie," their mother said. "It's jes' pie."

"There speaks the linguist," their father said, laughing, as they got back in the car.

Ariadne didn't feel like eating, but she knew that her parents would make a big deal out of it if she said so, so she just looked out the window as they drove the short distance.

Her mom pulled up in front of the diner. "One thing about this town," she said. "There's never any trouble finding a parking spot." As Ariadne climbed painfully out of the car, she caught a glimpse of Mrs. Harrison through the window of the ice-cream store.

"Mom," she said. "I interviewed Mrs. Harrison for my social-studies project, and I need to ask her one more thing. Can you just order me some chocolate cake, and I'll be right there?"

"Okay," her mother said. "But make it quick. From what I hear of Ann Harrison, she doesn't like people talking to her."

"I will," Ariadne said, and pushed open the glass door of Fender's Ice Cream. Without looking up from the sink, Mrs. Harrison said, "May I help you?" Ariadne didn't answer, and Mrs. Harrison repeated, "May I help—" And then she saw Ariadne. Her hand squeezed the sponge, and dish water streamed out of it.

Ariadne cleared her throat. "I found her, Mrs. Harrison," she said. "I found May Butler."

eighteen

Mrs. Harrison just looked at her.

"I don't know what you're talking about," she said at last. "I don't know any May Butler."

"Yes, you do," Ariadne said, "but you don't have to talk about it. I just wanted to tell you that I found her. And I don't know what to do with her."

"I don't know what you're talking about," Mrs. Harrison repeated. "And unless you want some ice cream, you'd better go. You kids have tormented me enough about that."

"I'll go," Ariadne said. "I just thought that you might have some idea about what she wants me to do." Mrs. Harrison stood silently, her back to Ariadne, her hands resting on the counter.

At that moment Hector burst in. "Ariadne, Dad says to come and eat your cake," he said.

"Okay, okay, Heck," she said. "Tell him I'll be right there."

"He said 'now,' and he meant it."

"All *right*! I'm coming," she said. "Get out of here."

Hector left but stood outside the glass door, gesturing to her.

"I'm going," Ariadne said, and moved toward the door. Mrs. Harrison said something.

"What?" Ariadne asked.

"I said," Mrs. Harrison repeated, just a little louder, "I said that a restless spirit has to come home, to be buried along with her kin."

"Do you think that's what she wants? And where are her kin buried? Do you mean in the cemetery outside, under that big rock?"

Hector's gestures became frantic, and through the plate-glass window Ariadne saw her father approaching. "I've got to go," she said quickly, and let herself out the door. Her father stopped when he saw her coming, and then turned back to the diner with her.

"I've never seen you so enthusiastic about a school project," he said as she slid into the booth next to Hector. Her parents looked out of place at the Formica table in their party clothes. She bit into her cake, her teeth aching at the sweetness of the icing. It was perfect. "What exactly are you working on?" he asked.

"It's about life in the valley and what changed when the dam was built," she said around a mouthful. "It's kind of about what parts of the old ways got lost."

"Like what?" her mother asked.

"Like this one old man said, they used to play music and dance in the evenings, instead of watching TV," she said. "And they used to tell all sorts of stories. So I found out about one of the stories, and I'm asking people who grew up here if they know it, people of different ages, and that way I can find out when the story died."

"And what have you found out so far?"

"Well, that old man obviously knew the story, but Caroline and her sister don't, so I'm thinking that maybe people born after the dam never heard it. That would mean that it had to be the dam that killed the story, wouldn't it?"

"I don't know, Addy," said her father, stealing a smear of icing off her plate. "Radio came around just about the same time as the dam, so maybe that had something to do with it."

"I'm not saying it was all the dam," she said. "The dam was just one of the—one of the—"

"Contributing factors," her mother finished for her.

"Exactly," Ariadne said. "Anyway, I found out about some neat places, some rocks with special names that look different from the lake than they do from higher up. Like one they call the bear. They say that you can only see it from our side of the lake, and that from below, like if you're on the water, it disappears. And I read about one that looks like an Indian chief from the left but a pine tree from the right. So I was wondering if I could go out in the rowboat tomorrow after school and look at them from below and see what they look like, and maybe take some pictures. And then I could take some pictures from farther away when they look like what they're named for." She held her breath. It was pretty lame, but maybe her parents would be so thrilled that she was getting interested in the area that they'd buy it.

"Sure," her father said. "I'd like an afternoon on the lake."

"No," Ariadne said, so quickly that her father looked hurt. "I mean, thanks, Dad, but you don't know where to go."

"You know you can't go out on the lake by yourself," her mother said.

Hector made a choking noise. Ariadne thumped him on the back, a little harder than necessary, and said, "Now, Hector, chew your food more carefully." She glared at him, and luckily he took the hint and said, "Can I have some more Coke to wash down my cake, Mom?"

"You can have milk from now on," their mother said. "One Coke is plenty." Hector made a choking noise again.

"Mom?" Ariadne asked. "About going out on the lake? Actually, I was thinking of asking Caroline's sister, Jade. She grew up here, so I bet she knows about the bear. She's a senior. If she can do it, can you talk to her mom and find out if she's someone you'd trust in an emergency?"

"I want to go!" Hector said.

"No," Ariadne said. "This is a school project. I don't want you messing it up."

"How would he mess it up?" her mother asked.

"Please, Mom," Ariadne said. "I don't want him to come."

"But you'd be dead if it wasn't for me—"

"Shut *up*, Hector," said Ariadne, and the fury in her voice was enough to make him be quiet.

"No, you can't go along," their mother said.

"Why not?" Hector whined, and their father said, "I'll take you out on the lake another time, and we'll both improve our fly-fishing technique, okay?"

"Okay," Hector muttered.

"So can I call Jade and see if she can go, and you can talk to her mom?" Ariadne asked.

"All right," her mother said. "Now eat up."

Ariadne finished her cake, half of Hector's, and their mother's lemon meringue pie. When she was full, she suddenly felt so sleepy that she crossed her arms on the table and rested her head while her parents had their coffee, and on the short drive home, she nearly fell asleep.

But as they pulled into their driveway, she sat up, wide awake as a realization zinged through her. She had to check something out.

She headed straight to the computer. "Don't stay on too long," her father called up at her. "I have to make some phone calls."

"Okay," she called back, and tapped her fingers impatiently on the mouse as the page on dams loaded. How old was Mrs. Harrison, anyway? Sixty? Seventy?

Finally. She found Cedar Point Lake. "Formed by the construction of the Wendell M. Horton Memorial Dam in 1951." So, when the valley was flooded, and May's old home—as well as Mrs. Harrison's and Mr. Frank's and all those others—Mrs. Harrison must have been about her own age.

And up till then, May had only been helping people. *She* had never asked for help. Was that because before the valley was flooded, she could go home? Had she been able to visit her old house and find some kind of peace?

If the old stories were right, some ghosts could go through walls and things, and probably could go to the bottom of a lake to visit their family. So why couldn't May? Maybe because she was real, at least partially. She could hold Ariadne's hand and take a stinger out of her finger and scoop mud into a ball. So maybe she couldn't go back down to her old home now that it was under water, just like a live person couldn't.

She logged off and looked up Caroline's number on the sheet that Ms. Saylor had given them. Caroline answered the phone.

"Hi, this is Ariadne," she said. "I hope it's not too late—"

"Where were you after school on Friday?" Caroline asked, without answering.

"I went to the library," she said.

"But we always go bike-riding after school on Fridays," Caroline said. "We waited for you, but you didn't show up."

Ariadne was glad that Caroline couldn't see her blush at the memory of her suspicions of the other girl. "I'm sorry," she said. "I didn't know."

"That's okay," Caroline said. "We can go next week."

"That would be great," Ariadne said. "The reason I went to the library was to get started on my social-studies project."

"Already?" Caroline said.

"Yeah, well, it's interesting," Ariadne said. "Anyway, your sister told me some stuff that helped me out."

"*Jade* helped you?" Caroline said. "I'm going to faint."

"No, really," Ariadne said. "She really was helpful. And I needed to ask her something else. Is she home?"

"You are so lucky," Caroline said. "This must be the first time in her life she got home from a date before curfew. Hold on."

In a minute, Ariadne heard a new voice say, "Hello?"

"Hello, Jade?" she said. "This is Ariadne, Caroline's friend who was asking you about May—"

"I know who you are," the cool voice said. "What do you want?"

And Ariadne explained about the cave, and about the bones, and about what Mrs. Harrison had said about a restless spirit needing to be buried where the rest of her family lay. All that stuff about May not needing to go home until after the dam was built, she kept to herself. She wasn't really sure what it meant.

"So do you think you could go out on the lake with me tomorrow after school?" she concluded.

"You really think it's May?" came Jade's voice after a pause.

"It *has* to be," Ariadne said impatiently. "Jade, I know it's weird, but think about it. It goes along with everything May said to you and me and Mrs. Harrison. There's a blue dress and old-fashioned shoes. It's got to be her. Can you go with me?"

"I suppose so," she said. "It would have to be after cheerleading practice, though."

"Fine," Ariadne said. "But also my mom wants to talk to your mom to find out if you're a responsible person."

"Put her on," Jade said.

"Mom!" Ariadne called. "Come talk to Caroline's mom about me going out with her sister in the boat tomorrow!"

Ariadne was too tense to listen, so she left the room. A few minutes later, her mother came out and said, "It

— 176 —

sounds fine. She's a junior lifesaver, so you can go out with her. Just swear you'll wear your life jacket every second, okay?"

"I swear," Ariadne said. "Thank you, thank you!" And she gave her surprised mother a kiss before running from the room.

nineTeen

It was drizzling when Ariadne woke up, and all day at school she kept looking out the window, hoping it would clear up. Finally the rain stopped, although it was still gray and windy. It was also surprisingly cool.

"I think you'd better postpone this outing until the weekend, Addy," her father said.

"Oh no, Dad," Ariadne said. "I really want to get this part of my research done."

"School's only been open a week," he said. "Surely your social-studies project isn't due for a while yet."

"No, it isn't," she said, "but I really want it to be good. First impressions, you know. If the teacher gets it in her mind right off that I'm an A student, I can coast the rest of the year."

He laughed. "Good thinking! But your parents can see right through you, so don't try it on us."

"I was just kidding, Dad," she said.

"I know," he said. "But seriously, don't you think you should call this girl and postpone?"

"I think she wants to do it now too," Ariadne said. Her father still looked doubtful. At that moment the phone rang. Hector called down the stairs, "Ariadne! It's for you!"

It was Jade. "My mother thinks we should wait until next weekend," she said, "but I want to do it today."

"Me too," Ariadne said. "Are you ready to go now?"

"I can be there in five minutes," Jade said.

"Great," Ariadne said, and hung up. She gathered her supplies: a waterproof disposable camera for taking pictures of the formations, so when she really got around to doing her project she'd have some illustrations, and a duffel bag with her dad's big flashlight and a piece of cloth in it. The gravel crackled in the driveway as a car pulled up, and she hoisted the bag over her shoulder and went out. It wasn't really raining anymore; there was just a heavy mist that stuck to her face when the wind blew.

Jade was standing outside her car, talking to Ariadne's mom. Even in jeans and a T-shirt she looked like a model. "You ready?" she asked, and Ariadne nodded.

"You girls be careful," Ariadne's mom said.

"I've been rowing since I could swim," Jade said, and Ariadne was surprised at her friendly tone. Why were teenagers such jerks to younger kids and so polite to adults? "We'll stick close to shore, and we shouldn't be out more than a couple hours."

"Okay," Ariadne's mom said. "I really appreciate how

you're helping Ariadne with her project." She sounded calm, but Ariadne could tell that she was concerned about the weather. She looked back at her mom as they went down the steep path, which was even more slippery than usual after the rain. Her mom was watching them, a worry-wrinkle between her eyebrows. The girls climbed into the little boat, and Ariadne settled the heavy duffel bag under her seat.

"This is too weird," said Jade, shaking her head as she buckled the life-jacket belt. "I can't believe you actually found her." She shuddered, then picked up the oars and pushed off from the dock. "I'll row, and you tell me which way to go."

"I thought you knew where the bear was," Ariadne said.

"Of course I do," Jade snapped. "But I'm facing back-ward. I can't exactly see where I'm going."

The older girl's familiar crabbiness was oddly reassur-ing. Ariadne directed her along the shore. It took longer than cutting straight across the lake, but Jade had promised that they wouldn't go far from land, for safety. Pretty soon the rowboat was floating in the same spot where Ariadne had tied up the day before. It was still gusty, and Jade had to work to keep the boat close to the cliff. In the wind, Ariadne couldn't feel the cool breeze coming from the cave. She looked up at the ledge. Could she really go in there again? But she knew that if she didn't return May's bones to her family, the girl would never rest. And neither would Ariadne.

She climbed out of the boat and said to Jade, "Just give me a boost, and when I get down there, you can lower the duffel bag after me. If you want to look around inside the cave, you'll have to wait until I'm back. We need to leave someone outside to get help in case something goes wrong."

"I don't think I'll go in there," Jade said. "I don't like caves. Just hurry up." She pushed up on Ariadne's butt, and Ariadne steadied herself with her hands on the edge of the cave mouth. She hesitated. The thought of going down into that blackness again, and seeing that small skeleton—

"Hurry *up*," Jade said. "Do you think I can hold you here forever?" So Ariadne hauled herself up the few feet to the cave opening, turned around on her belly, and stuck her feet in. Now that she knew what to expect, it was easy to keep from falling in headfirst again. Hector's rope was still tied securely, and she climbed down it.

It was even darker than the day before, if that was possible. She blinked and tried to make out her surroundings, but her eyes refused to see any more clearly. She slowly moved forward a few steps from the wall and stopped. The backs of her calves tingled at the memory of that underground lake in the back. Even though she wasn't anywhere near it, she felt that if she took a step she'd fall in.

"Okay," she called up to Jade. "You can send me the

duffel bag now." The rope scraped up the side of the wall, and the light in the opening dimmed as Jade tied the large bag to its end. She lowered it back down. "Why's this so heavy?" she called.

"My dad's big flashlight's in it," she said. "I want to be able to see what I'm doing."

"All right," Jade said. "Just hurry up. It's going to rain again."

"I'll be as quick as I can," said Ariadne, switching on the flashlight, but she hesitated. The bones were so small and thin, and the thought of May dying slowly in here made her shudder.

"Come *on!*" Jade called.

"All right, all right," Ariadne muttered. She took the cloth out of her bag. She had found it in her mother's sewing box. Mom would never miss it; she collected cloth wherever she went and never had time to sew it into anything. This was a flowered cotton, coral-colored—the kind of old-fashioned fabric that May would be comfortable in.

Ariadne took a deep breath and lifted one of the bones. It was lighter than she had thought it would be. She worked quickly but gently, trying not to think too hard about what she was doing. I'm just helping a girl get back to her family, she thought. Nothing more.

Her hand closed on something round and smooth. It was May's gold locket, still shiny after all those years. She shined the flashlight on it. The curly letters said, JBM—no, the one in the middle must be the last initial: JMB. Jane May Butler. Well, if she had needed proof, now she had it. She squatted back on her heels and pried it open with her thumbnail, holding the heavy flashlight with her knees. There were no pictures, just a lock of hair. Her mother's? Ariadne figured she would never know.

She put the locket carefully into her pocket. She'd show it to Jade and Mrs. Harrison, to prove what she was saying, that it really was May that she had found. She folded the cloth over the bones, the shoes, and the ragged remains of the blue dress. She made it into a packet to hold everything securely, and placed it carefully in the duffel bag. Then she added the heavy flashlight and tied the whole thing to the rope. "Okay!" she called, and Jade pulled it up.

In a few minutes the rope came back down again. The climb out was easier this time, when she wasn't all panicky and banged up from her fall, but it still took a while. When she poked her head out of the cave opening, she was surprised to see how bad the weather had become. Dark clouds were boiling across the sky, and waves were tossing the little boat.

"Hurry up," commanded Jade, who had the bag under her seat. "We have to get back."

Ariadne lowered herself into the boat and untied it from the cliff. The knot was wet and it stuck, and Jade jiggled impatiently while Ariadne fought with it. Finally, the boat was free, and Jade turned toward Ariadne's family's dock and started pulling on the oars. But they didn't make much progress; the wind was blowing them out toward the middle of the lake. The waves were higher now, and some even had little white tips on them. It was raining again. Jade's mouth was set in a grim line, and she was pulling so hard on the oars that her knuckles were white.

"Is your life jacket on tight?" she asked. Ariadne nodded. "Good," she said. "If we capsize, hold on to the boat. If someone comes looking for us, a boat is easier to see than a person."

Ariadne nodded again, her mouth too dry to answer. She didn't like to think of the boat tipping over and wished that Jade hadn't mentioned it.

They were tossed by another wave. Water sloshed over the side. She looked around the lake, but no one else was out in this storm. Her stomach lurched as they tilted and more water poured in.

"Bail some of that water!" Jade cried.

"What with?"

"I don't know—your hands!"

Ariadne let go of the sides of the boat and began scooping water, but it came in faster than she could bail it out. The boat tipped again, and she grabbed the sides to keep from falling out. More water sloshed in. "We're sinking!" she cried. Jade didn't answer but pulled the oars even harder.

The wind was pushing them away from shore. Ariadne could tell by the way Jade was twisting the oars that she was trying to get close to land, but the boat must be too heavy to move with all the water in it. The waves were growing higher, and the rain felt like cold, hard little hands slapping her face. She shut her eyes against the sting and the sight of the whitecaps, so she missed seeing the big wave that caught the small boat and then slowly, so slowly that Ariadne felt like they were hanging in the air, tipped them over into the lake.

Twenty

Ariadne's head didn't go underwater, but a wave smacked into her mouth and made her gag. She flailed her arms wildly, trying to reach Jade, the boat—anything, but all she felt was water.

Then something grabbed her hair and yanked. She struggled and gulped more water, trying to scream, but when she opened her mouth, even more water came in. Someone from the drowned town must be dragging her down to join them! She kicked behind her viciously.

"Ow! Cut that out!" Jade's angry voice cut through the sound of splashing rain and blowing wind. "Do that again and I'll let go of you."

Ariadne couldn't answer, and when she tried to nod she realized that Jade's grip on her hair prevented her from moving her head at all.

"Grab here," Jade commanded. "I told you to hold on to the boat."

"I would've if I'd known where it was," said Ariadne, wrapping her fingers around the hard edge. How could the lake seem so soft and harmless and boring one day and then try to kill them the next?

Jade didn't reply. "We'd better try to get to shore," she said.

"How?" Ariadne said. "Tip the boat back over? You were having a hard enough time rowing before. How could you make it now?"

Jade shook her head, and a long strand of hair fell over her face, looking like a piece of seaweed. She ignored it. "The wind's dying down," she said. "Our four legs will be stronger than those two oars. We've probably lost them, anyway. Let's kick together and head toward the bluff and tie up someplace. We can sit on top of the boat, maybe, out of the water."

Ariadne didn't know why that would be an improvement, but she didn't have the energy to argue.

She looked at the shore. Jade had said that the wind was dying down, but the brush that grew straight out of the cliff's face was whirling, and the trees were whipping around high up on the bluff. She couldn't see anyplace to pull in. Even if they made it to shore, where could they tie up? Wouldn't they just float there and bang into the rocks?

Then she saw a flickering movement on the bluff. It went in the opposite direction from the wind, so it couldn't be a tree, and—she leaned over, trying to peer through the driving rain—it was blue. It was a person. It was May, and she was gesturing urgently, pointing to a spot below her on the cliff. What on earth did she mean?

"Jade!" she called. "There's May!"

Jade craned her neck to look where Ariadne was pointing. "What?" she said. "May? *Where?*"

"Up there on the cliff! Don't you see her?"

Jade looked again. "There's no one there," she said, and started kicking. "And if we go closer, we'll just get knocked against the rocks by the waves. You're seeing things. Let's go down there and"—she gestured with her head—"and see if we can pull the boat up on that little beach thing."

Ariadne looked where Jade had indicated. It was a long, long way away. She looked up at the cliff again, but May was gone. Maybe Jade was right, and she was seeing things—there was enough water in her eyes, after all.

Jade kicked out with her long legs, and the little boat turned, pointing toward the tiny area of beach that Jade wanted to go to. But Ariadne was being dragged down by her wet clothes. Her legs felt like they weighed a hundred pounds.

"I can't kick," Ariadne gasped. "My pants are too heavy—"

"So take them off," said Jade, puffing. "I'll wait. We need to rest anyway."

"I'll have to take my life jacket off first," Ariadne said. "They're overalls."

"No, ma'am," Jade said sternly. "You are *not* taking that life jacket off, even for a second. Just live with it. We'll make it to that beach pretty soon."

Ariadne had her doubts. It didn't look much closer than it had when they started off. She looked back up to the cliff, and there was May again.

May gestured even more urgently, waving and pointing down to right below where she stood.

"May's back," Ariadne said, "and she wants us to go over there." She let go with one hand and pointed to the cliff that rose above them, then grabbed on to the boat as a wave rocked it and her.

"You're crazy," said Jade, almost sobbing. "That rock goes straight into the water. We'll be smashed against it. And don't let go of the boat again!"

"Jade, please, please go where May says," Ariadne begged. "Please."

Jade stopped kicking and bowed her head, catching her breath. She looked back at the cliff, then at the faraway beach. "All right," she said between gasps. "We can't make it to that beach anyway." And with an obvious effort she turned the boat and headed straight for the sheer wall.

When Ariadne looked at the bluff again, May was still standing there but had stopped waving. She had her hands on her hips, and she gazed down at them as they kicked toward the spot she had indicated. Something about her looked different, but Ariadne didn't have time to figure out what it was. Ariadne glanced back down to the spot they were heading for. There sure didn't seem to be any shelter there. But they had no choice. They had to trust May. Ariadne looked for her again, but all she saw were branches jerking around in the wind.

Then they passed under an overhanging branch, and the tip of the rowboat scraped ground, and they found themselves in a little cove that had been hidden by brush. Jade let go of the boat and scrambled up onto the tiny bit of flat ground. She grabbed Ariadne's wrist and yanked her out of the water with surprising strength. Together they pulled the boat as close as they could. The rope just barely reached to tie around the nearest piece of brush.

"She saved us," Ariadne said numbly. "May Butler saved us."

Jade sat down and hugged her knees, hard. She was shivering. "Maybe she was there, and maybe she wasn't, but we're okay for now," she said. "This cove must be way above the surface of the lake normally, but with the water level so high, it makes a decent shelter." She was tying the boat more firmly to the shrubbery that hid the cove. "Sit out of the wind as much as you can. We're both soaking."

"I'm freezing," Ariadne said. The temperature had dropped rapidly, and the wind was blowing hard against her wet clothes and hair.

"Come here," Jade said, and the two girls wrapped their arms around each other, sharing what little warmth they had.

"Why aren't they looking for us?" asked Ariadne after their shivering had calmed a bit.

"They probably are, but they don't know which way we went," Jade said. "I didn't tell my parents we were going to the bear, and your parents don't know where it is. I don't think my parents have your phone number, or even your last name, unless Carrie came home from Ashley's house and told them. We should have told someone where we were going. This is a pretty big lake, and there are lots of little inlets all over."

"And it's going to get cold tonight, I bet," Ariadne said.

"They'll find us before nightfall," Jade said, but her voice sounded uncertain.

"They never found May," Ariadne replied, and then she sat up in shock. "May!" she said.

"What?" Jade asked, but Ariadne ignored her and slid down the mud to the boat.

"What are you doing?" Jade cried. "Do you want to fall in?"

Ariadne shook her head and tugged at the boat. "What if the bag fell out?" she said, and started crying. "What if her bones sank to the bottom of this stupid lake?" Jade joined her, and together they righted the boat. But there was nothing in it. No oars, no duffel bag. Just wet wood.

Ariadne stared down at the boat. "All that for nothing," she said. "All those clues and falling in the cave, and then—" She shook her head and went back to the small shelter they had found earlier. Jade sat down next to her and wrapped her arms around her again, only this time somehow Ariadne could tell it was for comfort, not for warmth.

"We did our best," Jade said softly. "May wouldn't want us to drown trying to save her bones. She always tried to help people."

"Except me," Ariadne said numbly. "She didn't try to help me. I was just homesick and lonely, not sick like you or abused like Mrs. Harrison. I didn't need help like you. She came to me because she was tired. For once *she* was the one who needed help. She knew I would understand, because I was home but not home, just like she was. She knew I would know how she felt."

Jade nodded slowly. "That makes sense," she said. "That also explains why she didn't really know where she was. She was half here and half there at the same time, and neither place was really clear to her."

"She kind of knew where we were supposed to look for her, though," Ariadne said. "She must have remembered that she was climbing up that bluff right before she died, because she said you could get up to her, but not down to her."

Jade nodded again. "And she must have known she was right below the bear. She had grown up here, and even though it doesn't really look like a bear from straight below, she knew that's where she was. I wonder what she was doing, anyway?"

Ariadne shrugged. "Looking for berries? Getting birds' eggs? Something like that, I bet. She was supposed to be taking care of her whole family while their father was farming, and they probably needed more food than he could grow by himself. She must have had to climb pretty high to get to the cave, though. It's got to be way above where the valley floor used to be."

They sat up straighter and looked at each other as the distant sound of a motor reached them. But it became fainter instead of louder, and they leaned back. Ariadne swallowed her disappointment. Where there was one boat, there were bound to be others. Their rowboat was practically invisible behind all that brush, but surely people would be looking for them out on the lake, and someone would see the end of it poking out.

To take her mind off the possibility of spending the cold night in that cove, she went on about May.

"And after she—after she"—she still couldn't say "after she died"—"well, afterward, she sometimes came out of the cave to help people, and she noticed how it was cooler in the cave in the summer and warmer in the winter. That was the most important clue. Any of the old-timers who lived here before the dam was built would have known what she meant. It's just too bad she waited until now to say that one."

Jade gave a humph of agreement and stood up to look out of their little shelter. She came back, shaking her head.

"It stopped raining," she said, "and the wind is dying. These storms don't usually last too long here. But it's getting dark, and if they don't find us soon, they might not until morning."

Ariadne felt a twinge of fear. Didn't people die of exposure after accidents like this?

Jade must have read her mind, because the old scorn crept back into her voice when she said, "We won't get hypothermia, you know. Women have more fat cells than men, and we can take the cold better."

Maybe you can, Ariadne thought, noticing that even the life jacket didn't hide the older girl's curves. But I don't have any more fat cells than Hector, even.

"Poor May," she said, to change the subject.

"Yes, poor May," Jade agreed. "Stuck between two worlds like that, not belonging in this one, but not being able to go back to the old one."

Ariadne wrapped herself in a tighter ball, trying to calm her shivering. I know how she feels, she thought. But even as the words formed in her mind, she knew they were false. She didn't know how May felt, not really. May was dead. It was too late for her to join this world. But Ariadne didn't have that excuse. She could become a part of this new place while still holding on to the old one. Sarah could still be her best friend, even if they didn't see as much of each other as they used to, and it wouldn't be disloyal to Sarah if she made new friends here. May didn't have that option.

"I think May never really left this world," Ariadne said. "That's why she's more solid than ghosts are supposed to be. She took her mom too seriously when she said that she had to look after the others. She should have just stopped taking care of people, and gone to her other place, wherever that is, while she still could. And then her family all died and her home got flooded, and it was too late. She couldn't visit her old house anymore, where she had lived. She was stuck here."

"Do you think she'll ever get back?" Jade asked in a small voice, sounding younger than she was. Ariadne shrugged. She didn't see how, now that they had lost May's bones. Anything she could have done before—buried them in the village cemetery, had some kind of ceremony, whatever—it was too late for that now.

Jade pushed the wet hair off her face. "Maybe we should untie the boat and let it drift out a little way," she said. "Then maybe someone will see it. We can't row it anyway, with the oars gone. I don't think it's visible in all this—" The growl of a motorboat cut her off. For a moment the sound seemed to fade, but then it grew louder as though the boat had turned around. The girls looked at each other, and Jade leaped to her feet.

"Here, hold my hand," she commanded, and Ariadne grabbed it, holding on to a tree with her other hand. Jade leaned out as far as she could, with Ariadne bracing herself to keep her from falling in the water. "Help!" Jade called, waving her free arm. "Help!" There was an answering toot from the boat, and Jade retreated back into the cove. "It's okay," she said, and started to cry. "It's okay. They saw me and waved. It's the TWRA."

"The what?" Ariadne said.

"Tennessee Wildlife Resources Agency. They're coming to get us."

Within seconds the boat nosed itself into the cove. "Hold on tight, honey," said a large man in a yellow slicker, as he reached for Ariadne's hand and pulled her in. Another man wrapped her in a blanket as the first man helped Jade in.

"We didn't know it was going to get so stormy," Jade said. She was still crying. It was like she was able to hold herself together while she was in charge, but now that they were being rescued, she was falling apart. "It was just drizzling when we set out."

"You did just the right thing, staying with the boat," said the man with the blankets. "But we were told there were only two of you. How did that other young lady get up on the bluff there?"

"What young lady?" Jade and Ariadne asked simultaneously.

"The one up there," the man said, sounding surprised. He leaned back and pointed up the cliff. "Can't see her from here, but we spotted her from out on the lake. She pointed down this way, and then we saw you wave. How did she get up there from here?"

The girls looked at each other. They had no idea how to answer him. Finally, Ariadne said, "We didn't have anyone else with us. It must have been someone who was walking up there and saw us pull into the cove."

The man shrugged. "Can't imagine anybody taking a walk up there for fun on a day like this. We'll radio in for someone to take a look for her."

"You won't find her," Ariadne said before she could stop herself, but the man didn't seem to hear her.

The other man was turning the boat in the direction of Ariadne's dock. "Had no idea this cove was here, with the lake being so high. How did you know to head for it?"

Jade looked at Ariadne. "Just luck, I guess," Ariadne said.

"Well, I want y'all to give me some of that luck next time I go to Reno," the first man said, as he revved up the motor. The second man was on the radio now, saying, "Yes, ma'am, they're both fine. A little wet and a lot scared, but I wouldn't whip them too bad when you get them back." He winked at the girls.

Jade had stopped crying. She moved closer to Ariadne and said, her voice pitched low so the men wouldn't hear her over the motor, "Are you sure it was May?"

"Sure as I can be," Ariadne said. "She was telling us to go to that cove. And then she showed the men where to find us."

Jade looked up at the bluff.

"She saved our lives, Ariadne," she said. "She helped us again, and we didn't help her." And once more she started to cry.

They were pulling up to the dock. Ariadne's parents, and two people who had to be Jade's mother and father, were standing there waiting for them. Ariadne's dad reached down and pulled her out of the boat, and she felt herself enveloped in his hug. Her mother wrapped her arms around both of them.

I'm home, she thought, and allowed herself to melt into their embrace. I'm home. I'm not between places anymore. This is what home means.

In a moment, she pulled herself away. "I can't breathe," she said shakily, and her father laughed, his voice shaky too.

"My Lord," he said. "You had us scared, Addy."

"I lost your big flashlight, Dad," she said.

"Fine," he said. "Great. I always hated that flashlight. Thanks for getting rid of it for me."

"You're welcome," she said, and burst into tears.

"Come on," her mother said. "Let's go up to the house. Hector is having hysterics. He thinks that you sank to the bottom of the lake and have been eaten by those little fish. Let's go reassure him."

Jade and her family were already halfway up the hill. Ariadne let herself be helped up by her father. She stumbled into the house, and before she could get her footing, Hector had barreled into her and was crying, "Ariadne! Did you go back there? Did you get stuck in the cave? What happened?" Zephyr frisked around both of them, as much as a fat old dog can frisk, and barked.

"Hush," she said to Hector. "It's okay. A storm blew up, but Jade got us to shore, and some wildlife people rescued us. We're okay."

"But I thought you were going back to—"

"Shut *up,* Hector," she said. "We're fine. Really. I'll tell you all about it later."

"What cave, Heck?" her father asked.

"Just a game we were playing before," Ariadne said, and shot Hector such a fierce look that he shut his mouth and tried to look innocent.

"Go take a shower, sweetie," her mother said.

"That sounds so good," Ariadne said, and she went up the stairs. She was exhausted.

When Ariadne came down in her bathrobe, her mother said, "I forgot to tell you. Sarah called right after you and

Leslie went out. She has her reservations for Thanksgiving and wants you to e-mail her."

"I will later," Ariadne said.

Hector appeared from the kitchen, holding a mug carefully. He slowly walked up and gave it to her. "Hot chocolate," he said.

"Thanks, Heck," she said gratefully, and took a sip. Well, warm chocolate. Actually, cool chocolate. The mix was undissolved and gritty, and the marshmallows were like pebbles, but since he was watching, she drank a bit. "Tastes great," she said. He smiled, and she put it down when he wasn't looking.

"I need to make a phone call," said Ariadne, getting up.

"Not Sarah," her mother said. "E-mail her this time."

"No, it's local," Ariadne said. She went to the den and looked up Fender's Ice Cream in the tiny Taylor County phone book.

"Fender's," came an abrupt voice.

"Mrs. Harrison?" Ariadne said.

"What is it?"

"This is Ariadne Fellowes. You know, I'm the one—"

"I know who you are," she said. "What do you want?"

Ariadne told her what had happened. There was a long silence on the other end.

"I hope—" Mrs. Harrison started, and then stopped. "I'm glad you girls didn't get hurt," she said. Then, without saying good-bye, she hung up.

Ariadne sat for a minute before turning on the computer. When it had booted up, she pulled up the Web site that showed the before-and-after maps of the valley. She tiled them side by side and studied them. With her finger, she traced the route she and Jade had taken back from the cave. There was the bear, and there was her family's dock. There—she stabbed her finger at the screen—must be the little cove they had pulled into. She looked at the pre-dam map. Under the place where their sheltering cove now was, there used to be a few houses. Was one of them the Butler house, maybe with a family cemetery that had been overlooked when they moved the bodies from the big one by the church? Was May's old home below the spot where the boat had tipped over this afternoon, and the bag had fallen out?

If it was . . . how sad. May died right near her old home, maybe even just up the hill from it. Within sight of it, if she had been able to see over the edge of the cave opening. But nobody would have been able to hear her calling from inside.

Still, Ariadne hoped with all her heart that the Butler house—and its family cemetery, if there was one—was exactly where they had tipped over. Because that way her bones were now resting near the place where May's mother was buried, and some of her brothers and sisters, and maybe even her father.

Ariadne supposed she would never know. Even if

she did so much research that she got an A+ on her social-studies project, she doubted she would ever find out where the old Butler home had been. But for some reason, she felt at peace, truly at peace, for the first time since she had seen May Butler. Surely that meant something.

And tomorrow she would see Caroline again, and at Thanksgiving, Sarah was coming.

Ariadne walked slowly down the stairs.

"We're starting a game of I Doubt It," her father said. "Want to play teams?"

"Only if you promise not to sing 'We Three Kings,' " she said.

"Be on my team, Ariadne!" Hector said. "I'm the best liar in the family!"

"You bet," she said.

"I forgot to tell you that while you were in the shower, a girl named Ashley called," her mother said. "She wants to know if you get the math homework."

"I'll call her back after we beat you," said Ariadne, settling down next to Hector and leaning over to survey his hand. She knew she had done all she could, but still a wave of sadness washed over her.

She straightened up as a realization hit her. All at once she knew what had been different about May that last time she had seen her on the bluff. She couldn't wait to tell Jade.

They *had* helped May. She and Jade together had taken May home—she was sure of it.

Because although May had been wearing the same blue dress and heavy shoes as before, and the same gold locket lay against her chest, her face showed something new.

For the first time, May Butler was smiling.